A Savage Love 2

Aryanna

Lock Down Publications/Ca$h Presents
P.O. Box 1482
Pine Lake, Ga 30072-1482

Visit our website at **www.lockdownpublications.com**

Lock Down Publications
Like our page on Facebook: Lock Down Publications
@www.facebook.com/lockdownpublications.ldp
Cover design and layout by: Dynasty's Cover Me
Book interior design by: Shawn Walker
Edited by: Cassandra Barrett-Sims

Stay connected with us!

Text **LOCKDOWN** to 22828 to stay up-to-date with new releases, sneak peaks, contests and more...

Thank you for signing up.

Acknowledgments

All glory to God because He proves His greatness every day and I'm thankful for that. I have to thank my beautiful children, Aryanna, Micaela and Izzy, for being my motivation. I can't give you the world if I don't stay on my grind.

I have to thank my beautiful Belinda, to whom this book is dedicated to, for being my everything. I'll never know the darkness of a storm because you're my *Sunshine Bear*.

I have to thank my crazy family; Marvin, may you R.I.P., Monroe, Demy, Carmel, Ms. Gladys, Vinnie, Melissa, Tiffany *Smurf*, Kenton, Buffy, Monica "I'm back on the gas", Byrd, and Aniyah, just to name a few— I love y'all, real talk.

I have to thank my amazing fans who stay around even when I'm stuck in the lab, not dropping anything for months at a time; I do it just for you.

I have to thank everyone else who believes in me, and even those who still don't. One word: M-O-T-I-V-A-T-I-O-N!

Last, but not least, I have to thank my LDP family for still backing my play almost a year into this thing. All of you took a chance on me and that's something I'll never forget. And Cash, even though I get on your nerves, you know it wouldn't be the same without me. LOL!!

LDP we in here and the game is ours!!

Dedication

This book is dedicated to my beautiful Belinda for giving me the best year of my life. God gave me the talent, but you blessed me with your support. I LOVE YOU!!

Aryanna

CHAPTER ONE

December 2016

Ordinarily, the insistent buzzing of my phone would've killed my vibe at a time like this, especially given my current position, but this nigga's head game was average at best. So, I grabbed the phone to see what was so damn important at 2:15 a.m.

"Are you really going to answer that?" Ken asked, looking almost comical with my pussy juices all over his face.

Part of me wanted to laugh, but I kept my poker face on because I didn't need the drama that came with a bruised male ego.

"It could be important, boo, but you don't have to stop," I replied, hoping he'd do just that.

If truth be told, I really didn't care if the nigga got up from in between my legs, put his clothes on, and hit the door without a backwards glance, but there was no need to be cruel and state what I was thinking.

Kenneth was a good man. I mean, at least on paper. Good job, good credit, no kids, and he was actually a black man who loved black women; not to mention, he was six-feet-one, broad shoulder, mahogany complexion with dark chocolate eyes, and he was hung kinda nicely. He was also articulate, sweet and intelligent.

Meeting at a jazz club two weeks prior had been a surprise because not many men in their early thirties really appreciated real music anymore. I could go on listing his good qualities but as I scanned my missed calls and text messages, all I could think about was his inability to make me cum with his mouth. I mean, really? What grown man didn't know how to eat pussy? I mean, here I was spread eagle with this nigga lying with his face mushed in my sweetness, and all I felt was the roughness of his teeth biting at my flesh. Instead of licking me slowly and gently, the nigga was knawing on my pussy like a dog on a bone. Everything he was doing was all wrong, but I just lay there hoping like hell it would soon be over. Sure, I was wet, but the juices flowing had nothing to do with the act he was attempting to perform.

Granted, not every woman got to the top of the mountain the same way, but after fifteen minutes we should at least be seeing some peaks along the way! No matter how good a guy he was, if my sexual appetite wasn't satisfied, another would have to take his place. And based on the text asking me if I was busy, it was safe to assume another batter was stepping up to take a swing at the plate. I didn't know of no negro who would be sending a text asking if you were busy at two a.m. unless they were trying to get busy. Besides, the dudes I dealt with knew better than to come half-stepping or risk becoming a slave to this thunder cat.

If sex was a weapon then I was a bona fide serial killer, and I owned it proudly. No, I wasn't a hoe, but I did, however, know some hoes. I more-or-less categorized myself as a woman who fully owned her sexuality and all that came with it. So, any man who thought it was a game would become a casualty of war, just like the sad sight slurping at me without a sense of direction or purpose.

Now, the nigga texting me didn't need any maps or instructions on how to find all my hidden treasures. The only question in my mind now was how long it would take to switch one out for the other? I quickly sent a text back telling him I was suffering through some "bad head", and asked what he was doing.

Oblivious to what I was doing, Ken kept right on licking, but my mind was on Jerome and his thick ass tongue; the things he could do with his mouth should've been against the law, but of course you would never find a bitch to complain. He was only twenty-six-years-old and not much to look at, but he was a genius in the bedroom.

"Did you cum, baby?" Ken looked up and asked.

I looked at him bewildered for a couple of reasons. First off, if a nigga had to ask that question then that showed his lack of experience as well as his inattention to what my body was saying. And for two, this mufucka saw me laying there texting! Sure, I had offered the obligated moans, but I didn't want to over-do faking it because I surely didn't need him anticipating a repeat performance.

It was on the tip of my tongue to tell this nigga what was on my mind, but looking at him closely in the dim living room light, I could see his clean cut face was drenched from me. Thinking about Jerome made me wetter than I'd realized, but it also gave me the excuse I needed.

"Yeah, I came, baby, and I needed that."

"It's only the beginning," he replied, pulling me to the edge of my leather sofa, and grabbing his dick like he was preparing for battle.

"Hold up, boo," I said, sitting up just as my phone vibrated again.

A quick look at the message told me this was gonna be a long night. I knew myself well enough to know I was a lot of things and I came with a lot of shit. But, I wasn't a liar. Would I lie? Yes, especially if it involved someone I loved being hurt or worse. But I didn't lie to these niggas in these streets because I didn't owe them shit. So it was beyond me why this mufucka would hit me back and tell me I was lying. The nigga even had the nerve to tell me *he* was my man right before he bragged about his head game being on point. *I know this nigga didn't come at me like we exclusive or like the pussy belonged to him. My man?* I thought to myself. Oh nah, this nigga got life fucked up 'cause Shayna Blizz didn't have a man, nor did I answer to one.

"I want a picture to remember the first time you ate this good shit," I said, already snapping the picture and sending it to Jerome. I accompanied the photo with a text that said *have a good night*, and then proceeded to erase him from my contacts. I had no time for the bullshit.

"Did you take the picture?" Ken asked.

"Yea, I got it, but, baby, I'm sleepy now. You wore me out."

I could see him trying to hide the disappointment behind a smile of achievement, but at that moment I didn't give a damn how he felt. All I preferred right now was some me-time.

"Can I see you tomorrow?" he asked, with his hands still lightly massaging my thighs.

"Yeah, boo, let's have dinner or something," I replied, closing my legs and lying down on my couch.

He smiled and placed a clumsy kiss on my hip before standing to put his clothes back on. I admired his body until it was completely covered. He headed towards my front door and made his exit.

Once the lock engaged I took a deep breath and sat up, ignoring the insistent vibration of the text I knew Jerome was sending back. Hopefully, he'd take the hint quicker than the others who had fallen before him.

I took my Cherry Wood cigar box off the coffee table, took out a blunt, and twisted it up. It was too late for music, but I still needed to unwind and relax my nerves before work in a few hours.

Once I had my Dutch lit, I grabbed the book I'd been reading by Coffee, *Restraining Order,* and kicked my feet up on the table. I was so wrapped up in home-girl's storytelling, when I looked up again it was five a.m. and I hadn't even checked to make sure all my people had made it home safely.

As an entrepreneur I pretty much kept my own hours, but I still had to make sure my employees were on time for the next day's festivities, and that started with making sure they got home. Grabbing my phone, I sent out a group text before putting my book away and heading to the shower. Being in this world as long as I had, I had no problem owning my fifty plus years because I looked fabulous. I guess I was a creature of habit.

Stepping into my bedroom I looked over, longing to dive in my California king sized bed. I knew I wouldn't feel its comfort until the day's end, but I was already anticipating the way it held me close. Pushing the thought to the back of my mind, I quickly made my bed, loving the feel of my purple silk sheets sliding between my manicured fingers.

With that accomplished, I went into the bathroom, I turned on the shower, and let the water rise to the blistering hot temperature I love, while I finished straightening up my room. My color scheme was purple. In my opinion, there was no reason for a bitch to live in the Pent House if she couldn't do it right, and my pedicured feet deserved the same pampering the rest of my body got which is why I had heated, black marble that matched everything covering my five-hundred-foot bedroom floor.

Picking up the remote from the nightstand by my bed, I cycled through my music selection looking for something to suit my mood and start the day right. Despite the early morning bullshit, reading what my girl Reds had written had me feeling the power of my pussy right now, so I decided to go with that *Whip Appeal*. You could never go wrong with Baby Face and his fine ass! Mmph!

My next step was my walk in closet where I scanned the rows and rows of clothes that seemed to multiply whether I went shopping or not.

I'm not now, nor would I ever be, one of them skinny 'all I eat is leaves' type females I see on a daily basis. I got ass, hips, thighs, titties, attitude, no FUPA, and I wasn't scared to show it. Don't get it twisted though because I had style, and I carried all five-foot four-inches, one-hundred and sixty-seven pounds of this thick chocolate Goddess with it.

There were only a few meetings today so casual chic was what I wanted when I selected my cream Dolce and Gabbana knee length skirt, quart cut tan high heeled Gucci boots, and black sleeveless Gucci blouse.

I learned long ago that those with money didn't have to boast about having it. Therefore, my one carat diamond studs and the gold cross my mom gave me were all the accessorizing needed to complete my ensemble. With the hard part complete, I finished the morning ritual of bathing and putting myself together, before grabbing my purse and heading down to the lobby.

At exactly six fifteen a.m., I stepped outside and into the waiting backseat of my white on white 2016 Rolls Royce Phantom. Immediately, my driver pulled off into traffic, maneuvering with the speed and efficiency I demanded because Baltimore traffic at rush hour was a bitch.

"Good morning Mrs. Blizzard, what does our schedule look like today?"

"I'll be at the office until lunch, Antwan, and then I have to prepare for tonight's party," I replied, sending texts confirming appointments, and Facebooking a mile a minute.

"Ah, it is time for one of your quarterly functions isn't it."

As always, this was his play at getting an invite, but he knew how I felt about mixing business and pleasure. Antwan had been my driver for the last two years and we were cool, but owning my own business had taught me some valuable lessons. *Blizz Party Planning* was damn near a house hold name now and the last thing I needed was descrambled employees fucking up my business.

"You know the rules 'Twan," I said, smiling despite myself. *This is what I get for hiring my home-girl's eighteen-year-old nephew and letting him see what the shit in the movies is all about,* I thought.

"Yeah I know. It's just that my birthday is this weekend and I'm not throwing my own party so-"

"See, here you go," I said, laughing at the sheepish look he was trying to give me in the rearview mirror.

His ass wasn't black though, and I knew good and damn well he could've found some little hood rat or Becky to throw him a party, eat his dick up and whatever else he desired. He had the little light skin pretty boy swag working and what not, and working for me, his attire had to be fresh, always. So there really was no reason for the big, ripping dog eyes he was giving me.

I went back to handling business on both of the phones in my hand, ignoring him for the moment as everybody checked in before the day started. By the time we pulled up in front of my office building in Northwest DC, there was only one person I hadn't heard from.

"Did you drive Alicia last night?" I asked Twan. While he was my personal driver, once I was in for the night, I didn't mind my closest hoe-girls using him as long as it was business.

"No, I think Travis took her to dance somewhere in the West end."

Travis was one of the Uber drivers we kept on personal retainer to move around DC, MD and VA. He was part of the team so I sent him a text as I hopped out of the car and headed inside the building.

As soon as I was thru the door, I pulled up short at the sight of him. Despite the divorce that had been less than amicable, we were on good terms, but I could tell he was in his official capacity which was a bad thing.

"What is it?" I asked, walking up, taking his arm to steer him towards the elevator.

"We got a problem. Alicia's dead."

CHAPTER TWO

My offices took up the entire fifth floor in one of Georgetown's more prestigious buildings, making it easier to cater to the upscale clientele I had, and justifying my prices. Ordinarily, I would've never dragged a cop through my office, or let him in voluntarily, but today, exceptions had to be made.

As we stepped off the elevator and through the frost covered doors that had the word *'Blizz'* on them, I could feel everyone in the room tense up.

"Pineapples," I said, using the security code word and taking Cliff's hand, damn near dragging him to my office.

As soon as I had him through the door, I closed it, locked it, and closed the curtains on the hundreds of eyes on the other side wondering what the hell I was doing with a cop. Of course a few people knew he was my ex, but it was still hard to see past his DC P.D. uniform at a time like this.

"Was it really necessary for you to come here dressed like that?" I asked, sitting my purse on my desk in exchange for the bottle of Cognac I always kept close.

"Think about what I just said, Shayna, and then ask me that dumb ass question again."

I fixed him with a look that should've made his nuts shrivel, but he'd long ago become impervious to that so I went right ahead fixing me a shot.

"What happened?" I asked, while the scorching liquid worked its way into my system and soothed my raw nerves.

"She was found floating in the Potomac a couple hours ago, overdosed on molly."

"Molly? When the fuck did she start fucking with that shit?"

"I don't know, thought maybe you'd introduced her to it," he replied with a smirk.

"Boy, please. I blow loud and drink, but you ain't never known me to be on no drugs, so don't start your shit."

"Yeah, a'ight. Where was she last night?" he asked suspiciously.

"I don't know. I'm waiting on Travis to hit me back now because that's who I heard was driving her."

"Okay, well, if he doesn't respond soon I'ma go see him myself."

"Do whatever you feel. Was she hurt or anything?" I asked holding my breath. It was a very real fear because the world was filled with crazies, and some niggas just loved to *take* pussy with their trifling asses.

"There was intercourse, but it appears consensual. How many appointments did she have yesterday?"

Sitting my glass down, I switched on my computer and waited for it to load up. You see, the truth was that my party planning business was wildly successful because it was really an escort service. We did legit parties, but like I said, I knew hoes. Fifty-plus years in the world had taught me that damn near nothing, except maybe drugs, sold better than pussy, and it would sell until the world ended. I was an equal opportunity employer, because you best believe I had those niggas out here selling and slinging dick faster than a ten dollar hit in the eighties or nineties.

I kept it cute though, and along with my "silent" business partner, who was now sitting across from me, had managed to build an empire that even the IRS couldn't tamper with. The death of one of my employees was bad because scrutiny was something we avoided like STD's and fatherless children. Our clients preferred it that way. I mean, shit, some of the world's most powerful people came through my city and when they did I made sure they had a memorable time.

Once the system was booted I checked Alicia's schedule and saw she'd actually had a free night, which was incredible luck on our end.

"She was off last night and had requested the first part of today off too." I said.

"Sounds personal," he replied, scratching his chin.

It was amazing that after all of these years, including the fifteen we'd been married and the five we'd been divorced, I still knew what his mannerisms meant. For a lot of men, the chin scratch was indicative of heavy contemplation, but for this negro it meant he was thinking about sex.

"Is whoever handling the investigation a friend?" I asked, hoping to re-center his thoughts on the situation at hand.

"Yeah, I'll be kept in the loop," he replied, sheepishly dropping his head in defeat. He knew he'd been caught having devious thoughts. "You look good today."

"Bye, Cliff," I said standing to open the door for him.

"Damn I can't even compliment you anymore?"

"Of course you can, just can't stick your dick in me anymore," I replied with a smile.

"Damn woman you hard."

"So are you," I taunted, giving a slight nod to the salute his zipper was giving my skirt. Where most men would've been embarrassed, this mufucka proceeded to do a grinding motion toward me, unzipped his slacks, and his rock-hard dick shot right out at me.

"Like I said before, bye Cliff, and if you don't want that mufucka all over the internet I suggest you tuck it before you walk out."

He did as I suggested, mumbling something about not being ashamed, and left me to, hopefully, turn my morning around. I closed my door, but opened my ventilation blinds so I could look out on all my employees in their cubicles. The only sight better than this was my bank account when I checked my monthly statements, because I'd come a long way from the streets of north Philly.

My story was like so many other's before me complete with severe poverty, no father, and influences that were highly questionable. My mom held shit down though, working however many job necessary to give me and my hard-headed-ass older brothers the things we needed. I didn't know of a stronger black woman.

"Shayna, you've got a call on line one," my assistant said over the intercom.

A quick look at the clock on my computer screen showed that it was exactly 7:30 a.m. which meant my caller could only be one person.

"Good morning, you old bat," I said in greeting.

"Good morning to you, you old bitty," she replied, laughing.

Every morning it was the same exchange, but I knew I'd miss the days when we could no longer do it.

"How you feeling this morning, Mom?" I asked, sitting back behind my desk.

"I'm fine, baby, just fine. How 'bout you?"

"I'm good, ready to get this day done and over with."

"Stressed already, huh?"

"Yeah, Mom, but what else is new right?"

My Mother and I had no secrets so she knew exactly what my business was and how I ran it. That didn't necessarily mean she approved, but, at the end of the day, I was beyond grown.

"You still coming over on Sunday?' she asked.

"Yes, ma'am. Have you decided where you wanna do brunch this week?"

We had a standing date every Sunday for brunch and gossip, going back as far as I could remember, and it was still the highlight of my week.

"I don't know, baby. I was thinking I might just whip up something here at the house. How would you feel about some eggs, corn beef hash, sausage, waffles and fried potatoes?"

How I felt about all that good cooking was immediately echoed by the loud rumbling in my stomach screaming, *"Bitch, feed me!"* But my mind was already switching gears because mom was damn near eighty and she didn't just break out the pots and pans without reason. Something was up.

"You was thinking about whipping all that up, huh?"

"Mmhmm."

"What's going on, Ma?"

"What do you mean, baby?" she asked, innocently.

"Nah, don't try to play me because you know me just as well as I know you, so I'ma need you to explain to me what this big Sunday brunch at the house is really about."

All of a sudden the phone was full of silence, but I knew she was on the other end and I could wait her ass out any day of the week.

"Can't I just please cook for you, baby?"

"Mom," I said, letting her know my exasperation was right around the corner.

"Fine! Well-I talked to Rah and-."

"Un uh, nope, don't wanna hear it. Next topic of discussion," I said, interrupting her before she could get whatever she was getting ready to say out of her mouth.

It didn't bother me that she'd chosen to communicate with my least favorite ex, but she could keep that shit to herself 'cause I didn't wanna hear it. As far as I was concerned, Raheem *'dog of all dogs'* Miles didn't exist to me anymore.

"Baby, will you just listen for a second," she pleaded.

"Momma, I love you dearly, but I need to get ready for a meeting in a few minutes and the last thing I need on my mind is him. Please," I begged of her.

"Okay, baby. I understand. Well, you go to that meeting and I'll talk to you later on, but try to remember something for me," she added.

"What's that?" I replied, curiously.

"One day you're gonna ask God to forgive your dog-ass too," she paused before continuing, "what if He doesn't wanna listen to you?"

"Then, I guess I better stock up on sunglasses and coconut oil," I replied, seriously.

"I love you, Ma," I said, hanging up just as my assistant, Melissa, stuck her head in my door.

"'Sup, boss?" she greeted.

"Girlll," I growled out in frustration, motioning for her to come in and close the door.

Melissa had been with me nearly since the beginning of starting my business, so our relationship was that of friends as well as employee/employer. Not to mention, she was a five-feet-two-inches thick, white girl with a handful of titties, a metro bus for an ass, and she could eat pussy almost as good as me, so we were definitely friends with benefits.

"Spill it, bitch. What the fuck is going on?" she asked, taking a seat across from me.

I quickly recapped the morning's events starting at two fifteen and brought her up to speed, still hating the way the nigga's name tasted coming out of my mouth.

"So was it any good?" she asked, once I'd stop talking.

"Was what any good?" I replied puzzled, thinking I had missed something. I knew she couldn't have been talking about Ken's head game.

"That new book by Coffee? I read *Love Knows No Boundaries One, Two and Three*, but I ain't downloaded the new book yet."

At first I just looked at her and blinked real slow-like before I burst out laughing. Leave it to this bitch to take my mind off of all the negativity and put it towards something we both enjoyed.

"That's why I love your crazy ass heifer, and you know that mufucka a page turner 'cause homegirl don't disappoint."

"I gotta download that then. Shit, I wish I could just download her thick ass!"

"See, there you go, you don't even know if she's playing for your team," I replied still laughing.

"A bitch can fantasize can't she? Besides, I'd switch teams and go threesome all day!" she said, laughing right along with me.

We spent the next half hour just kicking the shit, not stressing over the world and its drama for the moment, but instead, enjoying each other's company until it was time for the meeting I'd told my mom about.

"A'ight, slim, let's get to work," I said, standing up, and grabbing my phones.

It wasn't until I looked at my iphone that I noticed a missed call and message stamped urgent.

"I'll meet you there," I told Melissa, logging into my voicemail. I didn't recognize the number from the call I'd missed, but that didn't mean anything because most of my clients traveled the globe regularly.

"I don't have to tell you who this is because I'm sure you haven't forgotten. I'm in town and I was hoping we could talk so-."

I hit the erase button so hard I thought I was gonna break my damn phone.

"Motherfucker!" I exclaimed, fiercely, beyond pissed that he'd have the goddamn balls to call my phone after the shit he'd done. I didn't understand why this nigga couldn't just leave me the fuck alone. *I mean, three years of silence after I gave you detailed directions to hell. Was that not enough of a clue?* I thought to myself in frustration. Maybe he needed me to spell it out for him one last time. I damn near had his whole number dialed when a tap on the door diverted my attention.

"Hey, beautiful, you ready for the meeting?" he asked, giving me that mega-watt, panty-dropper smile that had made him worth more than six figures plying his trade.

The *he* in question was Marcus, aka God's Gift, and he was the leading male escort on my roster. Standing six foot six inches, weighing two-hundred and fifty pounds with a toffee complexion, you could bet your ass he'd earned his name. But, the way he was hung you might not wanna bet your ass.

"Come in for a second, Mark, and close the door."

I could see the worry in his eyes, but I was pretty sure it was because he could sense something was wrong with me. I crossed over to my window again and closed my blinds, as I prepared to break one of my own cardinal rules.

"What's wrong, Shay?" he asked, taking the chair Melissa had recently vacated.

My office was spacious with a huge oak desk that sat in the middle, with two plush high backed chairs opposite my hand toiled Italian leather swivel. With everything vertically digital and online, I only had a need for one filing cabinet that was the same oak as my desk, and it sat in a corner behind me. The rest of the space was occupied by my leather love seat that sat in front of the window, which meant I really had a lot of room to maneuver. But, whenever he was in here my office felt like a shoe box.

"I need a favor, Mark, but you can't ask any questions and it has to stay between us."

"Okay," he agreed without hesitation.

I searched his eyes for uncertainty, but all I found was curiosity amongst their green hue. Trust wasn't an issue because if it were, he wouldn't work for me at all. I was actually questioning how stupid I was, and asking myself was I really considering saying what was on the tip of my tongue. One look back at the phone in my hand answered my question, I had to get this nigga off my mind. I tossed the phone on my desk and stood right in front of him.

"Fuck me."

"What?"

"You heard what I said."

"I did, but just to make sure I want you to repeat it."

The time for words was over and done with. So, I lifted my skirt all the way up to my waist, and then sat on my desk, spreading my thick thighs to reveal my shaved, juicy pussy. I saw his mouth water as his eyes took all of me in, and I knew how bad he wanted it. Shit, if I was gonna be real about it, I'd have to admit, I had been wanting to give him some, however, I didn't wanna mix business with pleasure— until now, that is.

To his credit he didn't do what a lot of niggas would have done in this situation. Most niggas would've asked a dumb ass question, or just opened their mouths to speak in general. But not him. Instead, he stood up, dropped his slacks, and stepped in between my legs holding eleven inches of mayhem that he damn sure knew how to use.

"Remember, you asked for this," he said huskily, pushing his dick right up against my pussy lips.

"Remember who you're fucking with," I told him, as I locked my legs behind him, and pulled him all the way inside me, fast and hard.

Aryanna

CHAPTER THREE

The little voice in my head was telling me I was a nothin'-ass bitch, because instead of mourning the loss of an employee, I was now in my bathroom wiping cum from in between my legs. I could admit I was emotionally fucked up.

On the one hand, Alicia's death was part of the game and her own stupidity for fucking with drugs. But, on the other hand, indirect contact with Raheem had just caused me to throw my principles out the window. I hated that nigga enough to scream, but on the rare occasion when he crossed my mind on a late night, I had to admit the hate only masked the hurt. A psychologist once suggested that the hurt was masking the love; needless to say, that was our last appointment.

Pushing the thoughts of Raheem from my mind I finished cleaning myself up and stepped back into my office, where I took another shot of cognac. I wasn't paid to cum, only to leave. I couldn't fight the smile on my face as I walked out of my office and made my way towards the conference room. Marcus had actually thought I couldn't handle him, but he learned very quickly the power of the p-u-s-s-y. In the end, I promised to never tell anyone that I'd made him my bitch, and even offered to give him a run-back when he was ready.

Voices quieted and all eyes turned in my direction when I breezed through the door. I ran my business something like the NBA in the sense that you had the regular league and the development league. This meeting consisted of my top earners which left all D-league players out, but the important things were passed along accordingly. I did hold occasional meetings with the D-league, but only when they earned the right to be in my presence.

Right now there were approximately thirty to forty sets of eyes on me, all seated around my maple wood conference table, which took up the room almost wall to wall. Part of me knew it wasn't right to take pride in the type of work I was doing, but the other part of me knew it took a bad bitch to run an empire. To know *I* was that bitch made my sweet spot tingle even more than the fresh memories of Marcus being deep inside me.

"Listen up," I ordered, taking my seat at the head of the table, and accepting the cup of coffee Melissa handed me.

"I know the sight of a cop panicked a lot of you, but that particular cop just happens to be my ex-husband. However, as it is with any cop, he didn't come with good news. Alicia's body was found in the Potomac river this morning and apparently she'd overdosed on molly."

I could see the look of fear in almost everyone's eyes when they heard Alicia was dead, but that fear shifted to shock when I revealed *how* she died. I tried not to judge, but it was seriously beyond me why this generation wanted to fuck with drugs when they couldn't even pronounce the ingredients, let alone spell them! I, myself smoked weed. Shit, even my mom had smoked weed back in her day and there wasn't shit wrong with that. All the rest of that chemically enhanced bullshit was for the birds though, and I definitely didn't play that shit if you were on my payroll. "Everybody in here is grown, which means you make your own decisions, but you know my rules. If I find out any of you are fucking around, then you'll find yourself on the wrong side of my friendship. As soon as the cops release her body we'll start planning a service for her that's fit for a queen. I'll let you know when to clear your schedules.

In the meantime, I'm postponing tonight's party for obvious reasons, but I won't stop anyone who wants to take dates and make money. Speaking of which, Alicia had requested last night and this morning off, do any of you know why?" I questioned, as I looked from one face to another.

It wasn't mandatory that everybody be up in everybody's business, but I tried to keep shit tight knit like a family, especially since most of them didn't have one. Scanning the room, I caught a lot of negative shakes of heads and I heard others mumbling their ignorance of her where-about. But, as my eyes skated over Trish I caught that look of fear again. She knew something, but putting her on the spot in front of everyone wasn't how you inspired trust.

"Okay, let's get this meeting started. Ladies first," I said, ending one topic, moving on to another.

We spent the next hour going through dates, and business opportunities presenting themselves in the immediate future, and concluding with the weekly piss tests which were mandatory.

It wasn't a secret that I took my no drug policy seriously, and I wasn't a baseball fan, so one strike would get a mufucka gone. Once I'd adjourned the meeting I pulled Trish to the side and told her to go wait for me in my office. Whatever she knew had her nervous as hell, but I could see the appreciation in her eyes for my decision to handle the situation in private.

"Boss, you need me for anything?" Melissa asked, stepping to my side.

"Yeah, I need you to get the word out about tonight's cancellation. Explain it away as a family emergency, but don't tell anyone that one of ours died."

"When do you think you'll reschedule?" Marcus asked, joining us at the head of the table.

"I thought you weren't gonna do the party?" Melissa said before I could respond.

"I changed my mind," he answered her, but never took his eyes off of me.

This was exactly why I didn't fuck around with the help! This nigga was obviously about to let a five-minute freak session go to his head when he should've just been thankful and let it go.

"I don't know yet, Mark. I guess as soon as everything calms down. I'll add you to the list though." I replied with a look that would hopefully give him the hint to let it go.

"Thanks, Shay, I appre-."

"Are you bleeding?" Melissa asked, gesturing towards the bright pattern starting to spread at the shoulder of his suit shirt. My horrified eyes met his instantly because we both knew that was the exact location where I'd sunk my teeth into him when I came.

"Scratched it with a dumbbell this morning," he replied, hastily pulling on his suit jacket, trying to hide his smile.

"Take care of that, Marcus. Melissa's with me," I ordered, leaving the room with purposeful strides.

"Oooh bitch," Melissa whispered, laughing as we retracted the steps to my office.

"I don't know what you're talking about, and even if I did know this definitely ain't the place for that convo."

"Okay, but don't think you're getting away with anything 'cause I'ma grill your ass sooner or later."

"Agreed. For now, I need you to find out when we'll have Alicia's body, and make sure you send everyone apology gifts for us cancelling the party."

"You got it," she answered.

I opened my office door to find Trish sitting on the leather loveseat fidgeting with her finger nails. Trish was beautiful, only twenty-one-years-old with flawless porcelain skin, framed by stunning red hair that not even money could buy. Five foot even and petite, she was highly requested in the land of school girl fantasies, but she was far from naïve. Closing my door, I took the seat behind my desk before turning my full attention on her.

"What's up, Trish?"

"N-nothing, Shayna, just a little shakin' up about what happened to Alicia.

Did you know she was poppin' molly?"

"No. She didn't even smoke and only had a drink occasionally, so hearing that she was poppin' pills is a surprise."

I watched her in silence for a moment trying to see if she was bullshitting me, but she seemed sincere.

"When was the last time you talked to her?" I asked.

"Uh, yesterday evening sometime. She asked me to borrow those diamond studs I wore to the Christmas dinner party."

"Yeah, those were some nice earrings, which means she was obviously going out somewhere. Do you know where?"

"Sh-she said something about dinner and going to a club."

"Okay, with who?"

We'd been maintaining eye contact throughout the conversation, but when I asked who Alicia was meeting, Trish suddenly found something interesting in her lap. I didn't mind giving her a moment to compose her thoughts, but after a long one hundred and twenty seconds, it became evident she was gonna need help answering.

"Trish, I could tell in the meeting you knew the answer to this question, but I didn't wanna put you on blast. It's just you and I talking right now, but I will warn you that I hate to repeat myself."

"She-she said she was meeting an old friend."

"An old friend, huh?'

"Well, they were friends and use to work together…and he fathered her child."

Now, it was my turn to be silent because the shit she'd just said complicated things on so many levels.

"Are you sure that's what she said?" I murmured, hoping somehow she was wrong.

"I'm s-sure. That's why I didn't wanna tell you because she explained everything to me and made me swear to keep my mouth shut."

"So, then, you haven't told anyone else?"

"No, no one I swear."

"Okay, keep it that way. Understand?" I stated with authority.

"I got you, Shayna, you know that. Can I ask you something though?" she replied, solemnly.

I knew what she was gonna say even before the words left her mouth, just like I knew denying it was useless.

"What, Trish?"

"Is Zo really her child's father?"

"Yes," I answered truthfully but short.

"And is he really your son?" she probed further.

"You said one question, Trish. It's time to get back to work, but I'll check on you later today."

"Okay," she replied, leaving my office quickly.

There were rules to the game, and Lorenzo was more than aware that he had to make his presence known when he stepped into another's territory. Had he done that though, he knew he wouldn't have gotten within one hundred feet of Alicia, or any of my girls for that matter. I swear the nigga was like a black cloud; wherever he went trouble was never far behind.

I scooped the phone up off of my desk and angrily punched in Cliff's number. I took little satisfaction knowing I was about to fuck up his day.

"Meet me at my house in fifteen minutes," I said, as soon as he answered.

"I'm on my way," came his reply.

I gathered the things I'd need to take with me in order to work from home, and put everything in my bag. I then called for my car before summoning Melissa.

"What you need, Shay?" she asked, coming through the door.

"Look, I'ma be working from home today, which should keep the police traffic out of here in case they have more questions. If you need me, you can call me okay?"

"I got you, you know that. Is it cool if I stop by later on?"

"Call me first, I might be dealing with some shit that could take a while."

"Everything okay?"

"Oh, it will be just as soon as I get my hands on this nigga."

"Be safe out there," she said. "I ain't tryna have to come bail your crazy ass out of jail."

"Wouldn't be the first time," I replied, chuckling.

After making sure the computer was shut down I followed Melissa out of my office, and left her at her desk before making my way down stairs.

***

"We taking an early lunch?" Twan asked, holding my car door open for me.

"Nah, I've got some business to tend to really quick so take me home."

As soon as I was in the confines of my plush leather seats, hidden behind tinted windows, I fired up a blunt and inhaled until I thought my lungs would collapse.

Zo's, presence would bring unwanted questions if the police ever found out he was the last person to see Alicia. Most cops had long memories, but DC's cops' memories were longer than most, so there was no way they'd forgotten who Zo was, or who

31

he ran with. Why this ignorant negro would pick now to come back up here from down south was a mystery to me, but he needed to keep his bullshit in check.

"Damn, you must be stressed because you don't never smoke in the car," Twan commented.

"You have no idea, and before you ask, *no*, you can't hit this."

"Oh, nah, slim, it's evident you need that one to the face. Just relax and I'ma get you home."

I did as I was told while trying to wrap my mind around the problems at hand. There were way too many uncertainties because I hadn't talked to Zo, but that was the first problem I planned to rectify. Pulling my phone out I sent him a text that told him to meet me at my house A.S.A.P., and not to bother trying to bullshit me by saying he wasn't in town.

Within a minute this nigga had the nerve to send me a screen full of crying emoji's like I was supposed to go for the idea that he was in mourning. That mufucka didn't love no hoes, not even the ones that had kids by him! I wasn't even about to entertain the thought of having a text or emoji argument with him. I went right back to smoking my blunt and trying to relax.

By the time we pulled up in front of my building I was nicely faded and somewhat optimistic about this little gathering I'd arranged, but once again, the sight of Cliff filled me with a slight feeling of uneasiness.

"You can take the rest of the day off, Twan. I'll drive the Range Rover if I need to go out."

"What about your party?" he inquired.

"I cancelled it, but if everything works out I might throw you a little something for your birthday."

"Cool," he replied, with a big smile as he got out to open my door.

I took my time stepping from the car hoping to hide the fact that I was amongst the clouds. But, when I reached Cliff, the look in his eyes told me I'd failed.

"You high this early in the day?" he asking, noticing right away.

"Trust me, when you hear this shit you might puff the magic dragon too," I replied, laughing as we made our way inside of the lobby.

Once we were in the elevator he put his hands on my arm and hip, claiming he was trying to steady me, but I knew better.

"I don't care how high I am you still not gettin' no pussy from me," I whispered in his ear. Immediately, his hands dropped and I laughed at how transparent he was.

"Did you call me over here just to tease me woman?" he asked frustrated.

"Nigga, please, we got bigger problems," I replied, stepping from the elevator once we reached the penthouse.

"Problems like what?" he asked, almost running me over when I stopped in my tracks.

"Like what?" I repeated. Then, I gestured towards the figure standing in front of my door.

I hadn't seen him in years, but I'd recognize him anywhere. Whenever I did see him I always had mixed emotions and a thousand questions that all started with two simple words, *what if?*

The fact that no good ever came from questions like that didn't stop them from flooding my mind, but the reality was, life was built on regrets. Jay-z said it best when he said, *'in order to survive we'd have to learn to love with regrets'.*

"Is that...?" Cliff stopped his words short and hesitated.

"Yeah. Your son is back in town," I said, answering the question I knew he wanted to ask. "And what's even worse is, I think he was the last one to see Alicia alive yesterday."

Aryanna

CHAPTER FOUR

Dear, M, I hope you're doing okay and staying focused. I don't have to tell you how close we are to finally getting back the life we want and deserve. I miss you so much, I can't even put it into words. What I can say is, that once I've got you, I'm never letting you go again—for any reasons.

I know I've never really opened up about how hard it's been without you, but keeping it all the way real, my world ain't never made sense. I know where the blame lies so please don't think I'm directing it at you. Regardless of what's happened, I'm still the man I am because of the woman you are, and I love you for that. In fact, I love you so much, I've got a surprise for you! I know you're shaking your head as you read this because we both know how you feel about surprises, but I promise you, it's a good one. I'm not telling you what it is, just know that you're not forgotten and neither is anything else.

As hard as life has been without you, I've still learned some valuable lessons, but one thing we'll always agree on is forgiveness. Forgiveness is a luxury for God; it's His divine will. But, man has free will, and it's rarely forgiving. I love you and I'll see you soon.

Love Always, J.R.

Aryanna

CHAPTER FIVE

"Tell me I'm not seeing what I'm seeing," Cliff mumbled with dread.

"Damn, it's good to see you too, Pops," Lorenzo said, flashing that annoying smile that made bitches drop their panties.

I didn't trust myself not to cause a scene right here in the hallway, so I walked past him without a word and unlocked the door. I heard their footsteps behind me, followed by the door being closed. I was already making my way to my bottle of Henny 'cause weed wasn't gonna be enough to deal with this bullshit!

"Zo, what are you doing back in DC?" Cliff asked.

"That's a long story," he said in a nonchalant manner.

"Start talking then, nigga!" I yelled at him.

"I'm actually glad to see you, Mom, but I didn't miss that nasty ass temper of yours."

"Lorenzo, you're trying my patience and working my god-damn nerves. We had a deal, and so far, it looks like your father and I are keeping our end of it. You know I love you, but if you don't explain why the fuck you're back I'ma slap you to sleep."

"Okay, chill. Down south ain't home and it ain't never gonna be home. This is my city. *My* city and it was time for me to come back."

"That's not how this works," Cliff said, sitting on the couch.

I took a seat next to him, but Zo was too restless to sit. I could tell there was a lot more going on than him just being homesick, and whatever it was, I knew I wasn't gonna like it.

"Lorenzo, you know why this ain't home for you no more," I said, with more patience than I felt.

"That was a long time ago, Ma."

"Do you think anybody has forgotten? You think her family has forgotten? Zo, you did some truly fucked up shit-."

"You think I don't know that? You think a day or night passes when I don't see her slitting her own throat? It's been fifteen years, and still, there's not a mufuckin' thing I can do to change the past. So I'm just ready to get back to living."

"But you were living well down south. I never cut you out of your percentages up here, plus you and Success expanded nicely." At the mention of Success's name, I saw him flinch slightly, and the look Cliff leveled at me said he'd noticed the same thing.

"What happened?" I asked.

"What you mean?" he replied, evasively.

"Boy, stop playin' with me like I didn't give you the game. I'm the definition of an OG, and even though I'm a woman my dick is still bigger than yours so save the bullshit."

"We can't help you, son, if we don't know what's going on," Cliff said.

Lorenzo paced in silence for a moment before finally sitting in the loveseat across from us.

"The truth is. . . I don't know what happened. I mean, one minute we gettin' money so many ways it's hard to keep up with it all, then it changed. I mean, the money was still flowin', but the love wasn't genuine, you know?"

I nodded my head, fully understanding the more money, more problems concept.

"We set up shop down in New Orleans for a while, almost five years actually. Lately, the streets have been talkin' and I could feel the change in the air, so, I did what I had to do."

"What the fuck does that mean?" I asked, even though I knew the answer. Zo simply looked at me with eyes that shined with determination and defiance.

"Please don't tell me you're wanted," Cliff said.

"Of course not, give me some credit." Lorenzo said in an insulting tone of voice.

"Credit? I should shoot you my goddamn self and just eliminate the stress and risk right now!" I yelled, almost hurling the bottle of liquor at his head.

"Where is he?" Cliff asked.

"I don't know. I ain't never seen an alligator turn down a meal," Zo replied, smiling.

I felt the knot in the pit of my stomach loosen just a little, and I threw down another shot, hoping to get it gone completely.

"So why didn't you call before you came up here?" I asked.

"Because, I knew I wouldn't be welcomed with open arms."

"Well, damn. Can you blame me? There's murder and chaos everywhere your black ass goes."

"Yeah, I'm like my Momma that way," he replied, with a devilish grin.

I didn't have a retort for that so I let it slide while trying to wrap my mind around what all of this meant. I couldn't let the fact that he'd killed Success take up too much time and space in my brain because there were more pressing matters.

"Why'd you contact Alicia?" I asked.

"Because I missed her and wanted to see her."

"Oh, really? Did you miss your daughter too, my nigga? Because now she's an orphan thanks to you!"

"I didn't kill Alicia, Mom."

"Zo, Alicia didn't pop no pills. She knew my drug policy. So are you trying to tell me that she didn't get that molly from you?"

His silence spoke loudly and it pissed me off even more to know I couldn't prevent him from ruining another woman's life. It might seem hypocritical of me for thinking that way considering what my own relationship to Alicia was. But at the end of the day, I offered survival instead of death.

"Look, she only popped one molly before we hit the club. We danced for a little bit then went back to her spot to chill. When I left she was fine."

"What time did you leave?" Cliff asked, switching into cop mode.

"I don't know, a little after 1 a.m., I guess."

"And where did you go?"

"Back to my hotel."

"Which hotel is that?"

"The Doubletree."

"Did you go back out at all?"

"Nah, not until 5 a.m."

"And where did you go?"

"To handle some business."

"What business?"

To this question he just gave his father a look that said *'next question'*.

"This shit is serious, Zo."

"Did you think I was playing, Pops?"

"You see, this is why you don't come into another mufuckas territory doing business," I said.

"Territory? This is *my* ci-," he started, but I quickly interjected,

"Correction, this *was* your city, but you fucked that up! In case you need reminding, I'm in charge now."

"*We're* in charge."

"Really Cliff, you wanna pick now to have this argument?"

"Point taken," he said, smiling.

"Well now that I'm back shit has gotta change," Zo said, stubbornly.

"Oh, yeah?" I asked, sweetly. He tried staring me down for a second, but quickly realized there was no way for him to intimidate me.

"Did you fuck Alicia?" Cliff asked him.

"What?"

"You heard me."

"Yeah, but you should already know the answer to that question. I don't know about you, Pops, but I ain't lost no steps in that department."

"Yeah, you're really good at thinking with your dick," I said.

"You too," he replied, sarcastically. It took everything in me not to put my hands on that boy. It didn't matter that he was bigger than me; I knew how to inflict pain.

"You two figure this shit out, I'm going to take a bath and ease my mind. Cliff, don't let him leave," I said, getting up and making my way to my room in search of a baseball bat sized blunt.

My hands shook in anger as I rolled the weed up. I had smoked half of it before I even begin to feel an ounce of tension leaving my body. With each puff I felt my mind expand as my third eye searched for the solutions to all of the current problems at my feet. The madness in me screamed to simply kill Zo, but no matter what mistakes he'd made he was still my son. I wouldn't win mother of the year for my efforts, but blood was blood.

A knock on the door interrupted my reprieve and I opened it to find Cliff standing there with my purse in his hands.

"It started making all types of noises," he said, handing it to me.

I took the purse and shut my door without a word. I fumbled around inside of it until I found both of my phones. A quick check showed one missed call and two text messages.

The first text was from Kenneth, but I wasn't in the mood for any type of company so I ignored that one. The second one, along with the missed call had both come from Melissa checking up on me to make sure I was okay. I hit her back so she wouldn't worry, and made sure there wasn't anything going on at the office I should know about.

After making my way into the bathroom, I ran some water in the tub and added my favorite scented oils, already anticipating the way my body would feel under the Jacuzzi Jets. I went back to my room and almost naked when my phone rang, so I grabbed it and carried it with me to my awaiting oasis.

"Hello?"

"What's up, girl, what you doing?" Melissa asked.

"Just stepping in the tub to try and relax. Is everything good?"

"Yeah, we straight. I was just worried about you."

"I'm fine."

"Shay, I know you, and if you did what I think you did then you're not fine."

"What do you mean?"

"Me and you go way back so when we do what we do between the sheets it's never against the business and pleasure policy. You fuckin' Marcus is another story."

"Melissa."

"I'm not throwin' no shade or no judgment, I just wanna know what's wrong."

I knew she was being genuine, but what could I really say. The truth made me seem weak in my own mind, but I didn't see how lying would help.

"I just needed to get that nigga Rah off my mind, and I thought Marcus could help," I replied.

"Did it?"

"I mean, for a second it did, and the dick was good, but shit is deeper than that now."

"It was good, huh?"

"Stay focused, bitch," I said, laughing.

"Oh, my bad. So what else is going on, damn?"

"Well. . . Zo is back in town."

"What Zo? Tell me you don't mean. . ."

"Yeah, my baby boy is back to reclaim the city he loves."

"Could his timing be anymore fucked up? I mean, why now, and, oh, shit!"

"I see you made the connection already," I said, shaking my head.

"No, he wouldn't kill Alicia."

"On purpose, I don't think so, but he did say they were partying last night."

"Girlll, shit is just a hot ass mess with him!"

"Tell me something I don't know."

"What are you gonna do?"

"I ain't got that far yet, which is why I'm soaking in my tub, gun high, and it ain't even lunch time yet."

"You want me to come over?"

"That's not a good idea right now. I need you to have plausible deniability."

"Say no more, but, bitch, you better call me if you need me."

"You know I will," I replied sincerely. I knew I could count on Melissa to come through for me no matter what, and that was a rare quality to find in a friend.

"I'ma hit you up once I close the office tonight, and in the meantime, I'ma send you something to help you decompress."

"Okay, boo, I'll talk to you later."

We hung up and I took a long pull off my blunt, high enough now not to really care about much of anything.

Turning on the jets I lay back to relax just as another text message came through on my phone. It was actually a video message. When I opened it, I found myself face to face with a very wet and pink pussy looking at me. The angle was perfect as two manicured fingers first pushed their way inside, and then, gently, parted the juicy pussy lips to give me an in-depth look. The camera angle changed and I watched as Melissa brought those same fingers to her lips where she sucked her own juices off slowly.

I could feel my own pussy start to throb and I immediately began to rub my clit while Melissa went back to fingering herself. It turned me on even more to know she was sitting behind my desk doing this, as her soft moans I knew so well echoed off of the walls. I knew the grand finale was coming, and I was ready for it as I stuck my middle finger deeper inside me, rubbing my clit harder. As soon as Melissa's pussy began squirting on the screen, I felt my own gush, with wave after wave of satisfaction.

"Don't worry, I'll clean up," she said, licking her fingers again and winking at me before the message ended. The combination of the weed and nut had me in a deep haze, to the point I didn't even realize my phone was ringing again.

"Hello?" I answered, smiling and expecting to hear Melissa's voice on the other end.

"Is this Ms. Shayna Blizzard?" The man's voice was foreign to me, and not because of the weed or his accent, but because I'd never heard it before now. The authority in his tone was unmistakable though.

"May I ask who's calling?" I replied, cautiously.

"This is Dr. Weaver at Greater Southeast Hospital."

"This is Ms. Blizzard, Doctor. How can I help you?"

"Well, I'm calling on behalf of your mother, Ida Mae. She's fine, but she did suffer a nasty fall and-."

"I'll be right there!" I said, springing from the tub and running into my room for clothes. Fashion was forgotten as I grabbed a Polo sweat suit and some Timbs, no bra or panties required.

Tossing my phone in the purse on my shoulder, I was out of my bedroom sixty seconds after receiving the call.

"Where you going, Ma?" Zo asked from the couch as I blew past him into the kitchen.

"I gotta go to the hospital," I replied, searching drawers for the keys to my Range Rover— this was the downside to never driving yourself anywhere.

"What's wrong? You want me to go with you?" he asked.

"No, I want you to stay out of sight until we can figure this shit out."

I found my keys, and as I was leaving out of the kitchen, I saw Cliff put his phone down. The look on his face said nothing good had come from the other end, but I had more pressing shit to deal with at the moment.

"Life or death?" I asked, passing momentarily to gauge the severity of whatever he'd heard.

"I don't know, they found seman inside Alicia's body and the toxicology report showed at least thirty pills worth of molly in her system," he replied.

"Well, that gets dumb ass off the hook because he said she only took one, and I know he used a condom with her because she would've insisted he did."

Cliff's eyes skated from me to Zo, where he leveled a questioning gaze at him.

"You did use a condom right?" I asked.

"Yeah."

"Zo?" Cliff asked. In that moment I saw something I'd never seen in my son in all his life. I saw fear.

"Zo?" I echoed Cliff.

"I used a condom, I swear."

"But. . .," I said, anticipating the other show stopper.

"But it broke."

"So what are you saying?" I asked.

"He's saying his cum is in a dead girl, and his DNA is definitely on file. He's saying he's going down for murder, and that puts us all in jeopardy.

CHAPTER SIX

The ride to the hospital was a blur and there was no telling how many traffic laws I'd broken. My high was blown and the taste of Henny on my breath actually made me wanna vomit. There were absolutely no words for the kaleidoscope of emotions moving thru me right now. But, if I did somehow end up getting admitted to the psych ward I would be surprised.

Pulling into the first handicapped space I could find, I hopped out of the truck at a dead run before the squealing of the tires had stopped echoing.

"I'm looking for Ida Mae Blizzard," I told the first nurse I spotted at the E.R. desk.

"Are you family?"

"Her daughter."

"She's in room 17, which is around the corner, and three doors down."

My feet were already in motion as she proceeded to give the directions, except now, she was talking to my back. My mother was my whole world and a fall at her age could've ended her life in a hurry. *What would I do without her?* I asked myself. The mere thought made me shiver. I didn't even want to entertain the thought of no longer having her in my life, so I pushed it from my mind as I rounded the corner, pulling up short just inside her room.

What I saw in that moment froze me my footsteps in the very spot they'd landed. I wasn't sure if I was breathing, but I felt a pain in my chest and my vision was getting lighter by the second. Was I about to pass out? *"Bitch, you better not!"* my pride screamed at me in defiance.

There my mother lay, her small frame almost swallowed whole by the big bed with its ancient security rails. I could seed her smile from here, even though it wasn't aimed toward me. The recipient of the smile was what had me frozen in place. I willed my knees not to knock any louder than the African drums that banged in my mind. Seated next to my mother's bed holding her hand was none other than Raheem Miles.

It had been more than three years since I'd come face to face with this nothin'-ass nigga, and I had wished all types of physical ailments to befall him during that time, but it was clear to see none of wishes had been granted. Even in his crisp Lavender Button up and black slacks, I could tell his build was the same, if not more muscular. His dreads were gone, replaced by a close cut that allowed full rotation for the waves gracing his scalp. The goatee was the same and so was the slight mustache that I could still feel tickling my pussy as I rode his face. The negro hadn't changed much at all, and the dripping between my legs pissed me off even more-so than his presence. Before I realized what I was doing, I had taken my baby 9mm out of my purse, and was taking aim at the iris of his hazel eye.

"Shayna, get ahold of yourself," my Mother ordered, sternly.

The trance was broken as I turned my attention to her. It took a lot of effort to shove the pistol back in my purse, especially since the nigga had the nerve to smile at me. *I swear,* I thought, now angry at myself, *if my pussy twitches one more time I might shot my damn self!*

"Mom, are you okay?" I asked. Although I was beyond worried about my mom, my attention was still on Raheem, at even at a time like this. I hated the fact that he had this kind of hold on me.

"I'm fine, but what the fuck is wrong with you pulling guns in public?"

"I was caught off guards that's all."

"Shayna, you should know I would never do anything to hurt your Mom."

"Motherfucker-."

"Shayna!" My mom yelled. The tone of her high pitched voice forced me to look at her, forcing me to remove the heat from my gaze.

I held back the rest of what I'd planned to say and gave my mother the respect she deserved. I made sure to give him a look that let him know our day was coming.

"You need to be thanking him," my mother said.

I looked at her and waited for the punch line, thankful that the *'bitch please'* on the tip of my tongue hadn't slipped out.

"Thanking him?" I managed to choke out.

"That's right. Ain't no telling how bad things would've been if it wasn't for Raheem.

"What happened, Ma?" I asked, finally moving to her bedside and taking her hand.

"Well, I was out back putting the trash in the alley when some little fucker rode past me on a bike and knocked me down. I had already called Rah to come over, and he showed up right in the nick of time."

"Why would someone do that to you? Are you okay?" I asked, angry enough to reach for my gun again.

"I'm fine, baby, just a little bruised up is all. And I don't know why some fool would do some hateful shit like that, but if I see him again I'ma let God sort it out. Besides, I done lived in the hood all my life so takes more than some hoodlum knocking me down to shake this old lady up. I'm stronger than you think I am, baby."

"Well, did the doctor say how long you have to be here?"

"No, not exactly." She replied, evasively.

"Mom, what aren't you telling me?"

At first, she didn't answer me. Instead, she looked at Raheem and gripped his hand tighter.

"You need to tell her," he said softly.

I felt some type of way that they had some sort of secret, but at the moment I just wanted to know what the hell was going on.

"Mom?"

"When the doctor was examining me he thought he felt a lump in one of my breast. He wants to do a mammogram."

I couldn't breathe all over again and that light headed feeling was back in a major way. I didn't notice the tears on my face until I saw the tissue box Rah was passing me. I quietly accepted it and composed myself as best I could, locking my fear away because there was no benefit to it.

"When?" I asked.

"Any minute, I think," she said, squeezing my hand.

"I'll be right here when you get back."

"Oh, I know you will, sweetheart, just like I know there's nothing to worry about."

I looked her in in her eyes and I didn't see the fear I thought I would, but the determination that had been there my whole life. The woman was unshakable and I drew strength from that. Squeezing her hand back, I gave her a little smile as a nurse came in rolling a wheelchair.

"You ready, Mrs. B?"

"As ready as I'm gonna get, child."

Rah helped her into the chair and I kissed her on her forehead before she was whisked away. With my mom out of the room his presence was stifling. I reclaimed my seat just to put some distance between us, but that didn't stop the flood gate of memories from opening like Pandora's box. I was taken back to the first time I'd seen him.

At the time I was kinda using his lawyer as my fuck buddy and I had stopped by the courthouse for a bathroom quickie. I walked into the courtroom just as he was presenting his reasons for a continuance on Rah's behalf, and I made the mistake of actually going all the way up to the front row seats. Watching the lawyer work, sometimes excited me, but when his client turned those hazel green eyes on me my only thought was 'fuck me'.

I didn't care how we did it or where we did it, just as long as he did it right! He gave me a smile that was three parts confidence and one part arrogant, and it was enough to get his lawyer thoroughly sucked and fucked during his lunch break. In under sixty minutes, I made that man worship the ground I walked on, but in my mind I was seeing his mysterious client. Of course, I used the fact that the lawyer was whipped to find out everything I needed to know about Raheem Miles.

I dropped him a letter one day, and so it began. He got hit with some time, but time equaled money and a bitch had enough of that to get him home in five years. I'd fantasized about breaking that mustang spirit in him, but that first night I experienced something I'd never had in all my years. I didn't think it could ever happen, but that nigga actually broke me.

We must've fucked on every surface in my penthouse, and any rules I had I'd tossed happily out the window. He fucked me in my ass with no lube because my pussy was just that wet. He came on my face, down my throat, even in my hair, which was something black women didn't play about. For almost ninety-six hours straight he tatted his name in this pussy, and for the first time ever, I knew real love.

I thought it might've only have been amazing sex, but he was thoughtful with doing little things like foot rubs after work, and cooking me dinner. I'd wake up most mornings to breakfast in bed, only after I'd been pinned to the bed while he ate me for breakfast. My family loved him, my friends loved him, shit, everybody loved him! He could do no wrong-- that is, until he did.

Every woman knows when something is off with their man. It didn't matter how slight it was, or how slick he thought he was; a bitch knew when shit wasn't all the way right.

Most men were stupid about cheating anyway because they didn't keep the same sexual appetite they were used to at home. Rah was different though, I mean, a real life energizer bunny. I'm talking, four to six times a day, and a bitch was lucky to keep her legs closed on the weekend. My man didn't lay pipe, he laid the entire foundation! If that would've changed my ears would've went up faster than a K-9 working the border patrol, but since it didn't it took me longer.

Truthfully, I didn't see it, or wanna see it, until it smacked me in the face. Even though we were, more or less, inseparable, we didn't technically live together. Why? Hypnotizing me with the dick could only go so far. I mean, I'd already done the marriage and co-habitation shit, and that had ended with the nigga trying to hit me for spousal support. And trust me, that was a valuable lesson learned.

Us not living together gave Rah a reason to disappear some-times, but when he started ghosting like the boogie man my Spider Man-senses tingled.

One day I decided to pop up on that ass, but in doing this, I forgot the one sacred rule about relationships: if you went looking to find something, nine time out of ten, you'd find it. I remember it as if it were only yesterday. . .

I knocked on the door real polite-like and out comes Becky with the good hair— some young Spanish broad with flawless skin, and curves I could see through her little house dress. "Can I help you," she asked.

My neck rolled so hard, I thought I was suffering whip lash in the days that followed. But, in that moment, I only had one question: *Who the fuck is you?*

Becky with the good hair proceeded to inform me. *"I'm Mrs. Rosalyn Miles, Rah's wife,"* she replied, looking me directly in my eyes. Now, see, this is the part of the story where the ghetto black chick hops on the bitch's helmet and does damage. But, however, I was lady enough to remember my beef was with him. True enough, I did fire off a right cross that put Becky to bed, but I refrained from sticking my red bottoms in her ass.

My next move was to track him down, and like the average nigga he was, he played dumb as hell when found him with some chick at his apartment.

I cut him off for a few days expecting him to beg, but seventy-two hours without that dope dick had me scratching like a fiend! I went back to his spot, and when I got there, I found the door unlocked and the place cleaned out. The nigga had vanished like a fart in the wind, only leaving behind a single picture on the refrigerator; it was a sonogram picture.

I lost track of the days, weeks and months I cried, but eventually my hurt gave way to hate. At times, I wanted him dead, and I even considered putting Lorenzo on his ass, but what would be the point?

Why give someone that type of power over me to even keep thinking about them? So I tried to forget him. I locked my heart away and got back to the money, looking at our time together as a lesson learned—an expensive, time consuming lesson, but not a loss, because I hadn't lost myself. For a while that worked, but at the end of the day I'm a woman, and that one nagging question remained even now.

"Why, Rah?" I asked, looking him square in the eyes.

"Why what?"

"Don't play stupid, nigga. I'm still not above shooting your trifling ass right now," I warned.

He actually had the nerve to smile at me until he saw me reaching in my pocketbook again.

"You sure you wanna know the answer to that question?" he asked.

I didn't trust my voice so I simply nodded. He looked at me closely, from head to toe, invoicing the memory of how thorough his touch had been on my naked flesh. I fought the shiver trying to work its way up my spine.

"It's complicated," he mumbled.

"It can't be too complicated. I spent over fifty thousand dollars to get you out of prison early. I gave you my time, my money, my body, and my heart. Why would you throw all that away?"

"For something you *couldn't* give me," he replied.

"Like what?" I asked frustrated, curiously and unknowingly. Just before he answered it finally made sense, but I still couldn't stop that gut-punch feeling from coming. All I could do was brace myself.

"A baby," he said softly.

"You never asked me to give you a baby, Raheem!"

"What would've been the point?"

"We could've at least had a conversation and explored our options at least," I replied.

"You didn't want kids!" he yelled.

"You don't know that."

"Oh, yeah? So tell me what kind of mother turns her son over to the streets of one of the most brutal cities in America?"

My mouth opened to respond, but my brain had already utilized the truth of what he said, and it wouldn't allow anymore bullshit to spew from my lips. I'd never been a good mother, other or any other kind of mother to Zo, and there was no denying that. The truth was that when he turned to the streets I was the one who encouraged hm. *What type of mom did that?*

"Tell my mother I'll be waiting for her in the waiting room," I said, turning before he could see my tears. He was the last person I wanted to see my shame.

Aryanna

CHAPTER SEVEN

For the next two days, I shut the world out and made my home my fortress. I checked on my mom by phone, but she had Raheem by her side which meant she didn't really need me. His words still haunted me, but I did my best to block them out by focusing on the millions of other problems in my orbit.

The only good news I received was that the semen sample was too contaminated by the river to be of any use, which meant Zo wasn't in jail, and my family wasn't under the microscope. The bad news was that Zo was still somewhere in town, which meant shit would get worse before it got better.

The only consistent in all this was business. Sex sells itself so that only left me the hard job of spending enormous amounts of money.

During breakfast this morning it had actually crossed my mind to hop a quick flight to New York and do a lot of shopping. Rich white people considered that therapeutic, but two blunts to the face made me realize why rich white people were crazy. Not to say smoking weed was the answer to all of my problems, but it sure did cost less than a pair of fifteen hundred dollar heels that I'd only wanna wear while I was on my back. And, so, here I remained, a self-made prisoner in my beautiful castle. It wasn't all bad though.

"You wanna hit this blunt?" Melissa asked, holding it towards me. I didn't think I could get any higher, but laying in the bed naked with her smoking, guaranteed we'd get to the next level.

"What's on your mind?" she asked, as I lay there blowing smoke rings at the ceiling.

"A little bit of everything, I guess. Shit is ugly right now."

"Yeah, but it don't stay that way forever, boo. You just gotta fight through the bad times to get to the better times."

"Easier said than done, especially with Zo being back."

"What's that about anyway?" she asked, her face wrinkling in genuine surprise.

"I don't know, maybe the nigga is having a midlife crisis. I don't see anything good coming from his being in DC though," I said, shaking my head.

"You want me to talk to him?"

"And say what?" I asked, sliding a quizzical look her way.

"I don't know, maybe convince him to leave and go further north."

"Ain't no convincing his stubborn ass of nothin'. If I didn't know any better, I'd think he came back here over guilt."

"Guilt?" she asked, puzzled.

"Yeah. What he did to Makayla and everything that happened after that ain't just some shit you can shake off. He didn't just lose her, he lost his son too."

"Is he still looking for his son?"

"I don't know. Even with all his power and connections he couldn't find out what Makayla's family did with him. And it wasn't like he could stay in DC and keep searching, because once her family put the word out about what happened, the city tried to swallow Zo. That's why I don't understand his return," I said, talking more to myself than to her.

"It's been a long time though, Shay."

"Really? Do you remember how to forget?" I asked seriously. My question was met with silence as I passed the blunt back to her.

No amount of time could erase what Lorenzo had done, especially since everyone loved Makayla. Truthfully, the only reason I survived this long was because I had elevated myself beyond the streets, and hid in the shadows of legitimate business. My son returning threatened to fuck up my business. Maybe it was time to retire, do some travelling and really enjoy my money.

"You ever been to Bora Bora?" I asked her.

"A long time ago, why?"

"I'm thinking it might be time for a vacation."

"How long?"

"I don't know, indefinite."

"Indefinite. You mean you're seriously thinking about walking away?"

"Why not, I got plenty of money. I can always get somebody to run the business while I'm gone."

"Somebody like who?"

"Well my first choice would be you, but I was hoping you'd come with."

"Bitch, you know you'd get tired of me!" she replied, laughing.

"Maybe so, but you know I got love for you, so we could always make it work. Would you hang up your stilettos if I asked you to?"

"Only if I could wear them for you from time to time."

"Of course," I said, pulling her body closer to me. As soon as she laid her head on my chest, my phone started ringing. At first I didn't move.

"You gonna answer it?" she asked, looking up at me.

"You're here in bed with me so that means whatever that call is, it ain't good news."

"Maybe, but how is not answerin' gonna change that?" Her logic made sense, but I still didn't reach for the phone.

"Shay."

"A'ight, damn!" I said, exasperated, snatching the phone off of my nightstand. "What is it?" I asked, snapping at whoever was on the other end of the recevier.

"Mrs. Blizzard, it's Leroy down at the club." Leroy was my head security guy at the playhouse, the club I'd taken over for Zo and Success when they'd left town.

"What is it, Leroy?"

"Well, ma'am, there's a slight problem that we don't know how to handle."

"And, that is?"

"Zo."

"What about him?" I asked, getting that *'oh shit'* feeling in the pit of my stomach.

"He's been hold-up in the office for the last day and a half with one of the girls, and honestly, we don't know if she's okay."

"Why would you suspect she wouldn't be?"

"Well, he started with one girl, but she wasn't into the rough stuff, and from what she told us, he was being extremely rough. So, another girl volunteered to go with him and we haven't heard shit from her sense."

"Who's the girl?"

"Trish."

In my mind I was screaming, *"Oh fuck,"* but I made sure to keep my mouth closed until I was sure what I wanted to say would be the only thing to come out.

"I'm on my way," I replied, disconnecting. I immediately dialed Twan and told him to get to my house A.S.A.P.

"What's going on?" Melissa asked.

"This mufucka Lorenzo is what's going on! Remind me again why I didn't have an abortion?"

"Because you don't believe in them."

"Goddammit, I'm reconsidering that stand-point right now!"

"What happened, Shay?" she asked, patiently.

I filled her in as I got up and got dressed, again, just pulling on a sweat suit but electing Gucci sneakers instead of boots. At least with these on I might resist the urge to get blood on them by kicking Trish's ass. Why this dumb bitch would choose to go anywhere near Zo was beyond me, but her ass was fired for damn sure.

"You want me to go with you?" Melissa asked.

"Nah, you can relax here 'cause this should only take a minute."

"Don't put your hands on nobody, Shay."

"Girl, please, we gotta plenty of bail money."

"Don't put your hands on nobody, Shay," she said again, more forcefully.

"Whatever," I replied, sucking my teeth and throwing everything I needed into my purse.

By the time I walked into the living room, the doorman was calling me up to let me know my car was waiting on me. I hid my eyes behind shades as I made my way down in the elevator, and out into the waiting backseat of my car.

"'Sup, boss, you look like shit."

"Fuck you very much Twan, and thanks because the last seventy-two hours have put some miles on a bitch."

"Yeah, I heard. Sorry about your Mom."

"Thanks, she's good though and her mammogram was negative."

"Kool. Where we going?"

"Take me to the playhouse."

"Do I even wanna know why you're hitting the strip club in the middle of the day?" he asked, pulling off into traffic.

"Not really, but the short story is my dumb ass son is up to no good."

"I didn't even know you had a kid."

"You're too young to know about him and his bullshit, but yeah, I've got a son, and right now he's a pain in my ass!"

"All I can say is he must not know you like the rest of us, or he'd know not to get on your bad side."

"Right."

We rode on in silence and I tried to wrap my mind around whatever awaited me at the club. There was no telling what the fuck had been going on for the past thirty-six hours, but for them to call me spoke volumes to the fear I assumed they were feeling.

"Take me around back," I ordered, as we got closer to my establishment.

The playhouse was a top-notch gentlemen's club in the city, with a reputation of good service and discretion, largely due to my choice of girls. I did switch it up throughout the week and let my men earn some of those dollars, but when it came to club, women made more money.

When we came to a stop at the back of the building I hopped out and put my hand on the palm scanner that gave me immediate access. My private elevator opened right in my office, allowing me to come and go unnoticed. In in this case, it allowed me to sneak up on a nigga.

Even before the doors slid open, I could hear Fat Joe and Remy Ma's song *'All the Way Up'* thundering through the speakers in my office. As soon as the doors opened I knew shit was out of control.

The air reeked of weed, and the funk of too much sex. Zo had his back towards me with Trish bent over my desk, both of them asshole naked and he was fucking the dog-shit out of her.

As soon as I saw the blood, I smelled it. I didn't know if the bitch was on her period or if he'd just fucked her until she was raw, but the shit was dripping down her legs and forming a puddle at her feet. Still, he just kept on jack hammering her, completely oblivious to anything or anyone. The combination of smells had me feeling sick to my stomach, and I didn't wanna step inside the room, but I had to.

First, I removed the pistol from my bag and screwed on the silencer I'd bought just for this occasion. I made my way to the stereo and shut it off, but the mufucka didn't even miss a stroke!

Before I even knew I was gonna do it, I had cocked back and clipped him across the back of his head with the pistol, knocking him out of her and onto the floor.

"Ah! What the fuck yo!"

"Nigga, have you lost your goddamn mind! I said lay low, not take a bitch hostage and fuck her 'til her pussy didn't work no more!" I yelled out in a fit of rage. I was now standing over him with my finger on the trigger.

"You trippin', she wanted to party with me."

"Does it look like she wanna party?" I said, gesturing towards the barely conscious Trish, who was still face down next to a quarter key of coke. It was clear her mind was lost somewhere in outer-space, but I couldn't muster up any sympathy for her stupidity.

"Get up, you ignorant, bitch," I told her. Her eyes rolled up and focused on me for a second, before rolling to the back of her head, as her body found the floor.

"Fuck!" I yelled, scooping her up and putting her in the leather chair in front of my desk. The first time I smacked her I did it lightly, but the second time, I brought it from the hip and she stirred.

"Heyyy, Shayyy," she slurred weakly. It was impossible to put into words how pissed I was. If this bitch was that thirsty for dick, she had an entire list of clientele, so why fuck Zo?

"Zo, get the fuck up and clean up your goddamn mess!" I yelled, swinging the gun back in his direction.

"Chill, Ma, I got it. This is my fucking club anyway," he replied, picking himself up and searching for his clothes. It was obvious trying to talk with any type of sense was useless when it came to this negro, so it was time for action.

"Lorenzo, listen to me closely," I said, putting the gun right between Trish's rapidly blinking eyes.

"What?" he said, facing me once he had his pants on. "I run this. This is *my* city. This is *my* bitch, and this bitch earns me six figures every year." When I saw that I finally had his undivided attention, I pulled the trigger, scattering blood and brains all over the floor.

"I was fonder of her than I am of you at the moment, so I'm gonna tell you this one last time. Get your shit together and lay low, or get the fuck out of dodge." Whatever he was opening his mouth to say was meaningless to me, so I tucked my gun back in my purse and made my way back to the elevator.

"Clean this shit up and get the fuck out of my club," I said, before the door closed.

I truly hated killing Trish, but she was dead wrong for putting herself in that situation. I could only hope for her sake the dick was worth it.

"Where to now?" Twan asked, once I'd slid into the backseat.

"Swing past my Mom's real quick."

During the ride I finally admitted to myself that this might not have been the smartest idea I'd had today. I was in a different frame of mind at the moment and seeing Rah would be the fuse to ignite my dynamite. Still, I rode on, twisting a blunt and lighting it just as we pulled up in front of my Mom's house.

"You waiting on me to open your door?" Twan asked when I didn't get out.

"Nah, just chill," I said, passing him the blunt. We smoked in silence for a few moments while I tried to convince myself I'd be okay if I walked in there. I'd heard people say if you told yourself a lie long enough you could somehow convince yourself it was the truth, but there was no way I could sell the bullshit I was pushing.

"Take me back to my house," I said, after we'd finished smoking.

"You sure?"

"Yeah!"

Without further delay, we were back on the road, and I was back to the million-dollar question in my mind of what to do next. I had to get Zo out of town. That wouldn't solve all my problems, but it would go a long fucking way to giving me a peace of mind.

***

"Home sweet home," Twan said, distracting me from my thoughts.

"What you getting into tonight?" he asked.

"I don't know, but I got Melissa with me so one of us will drive."

"You giving me the night off again? Yo', this ain't like you, slim."

"Life is crazy right now. All I can say is enjoy it because shit will be normal again soon."

"If you say so, boss."

Stepping out of the vehicle, I closed the door and made my way through the lobby to the elevators. On my way upstairs, I debated on whether or not I should call Cliff and fill him in on his son's latest stunt, but truthfully, I wasn't looking forward to even hear the sound of his voice.

I opened the door to find Melissa sitting on the couch crying.

"What's wrong?' I asked, panicked.

"Thank God you're alright," she said, running towards me and grabbing onto me.

"Of course I'm alright, why wouldn't I be?" I asked puzzled.

"Because-be-because of the club." Melissa said, almost in tears.

"What about the club?" I asked, shockingly.

"Weren't you there?" Melissa asked, confused.

"Yeah, I went and told Zo to get the fuck out, then I left. Why?"

"There was a fire, Shay. The club burned to the round." Melissa replied, anxiously.

CHAPTER EIGHT

"That shit ain't funny."

"Shay, do you see me laughing?" she asked, pulling me into the living room.

When I looked at the screen the news was on. Sure enough, what was once my beautiful establishment was now a banter of smoke and flames. I was seeing all of this through my very own eyes, but it was still hard for my mind to process it. *How could everything go from sugar to shit that fast? What if I hadn't left as quickly as I had?* So many thoughts began racing through my mind, and in that moment, I didn't have a clue.

"Did they say how many people made it out?" I asked, feeling a new type of panic and loss.

"No, the only thing they said was it appeared to have been some type of an explosion that came from the back of the building."

What I was seeing on TV didn't look like anything caused by a damn kitchen fire, plus, we weren't open for business.

"That don't sound right, I mean, the club ain't even open this time of day," I said, voicing my thoughts.

"I'm just telling you what was reported, boo. All that matters to me is you're okay, because I thought you were in that building and-an-and-"

"Aww, bitch, don't get all mushy on me," I said, taking her face in my hands, giving her a quick kiss.

"Whatever. You know you'd be the same way if you thought it was me."

Our conversation was interrupted by the ringing of both of my cell phones. As soon as I got them out of my purse I saw that one call was coming from Cliff, and the other was coming from the office.

"Call the office," I told Melissa before answering my other phone.

"Yeah, Cliff?"

"Have you seen the news?"

"I'm looking at it now."

"You need to get down here."

"Okay, but there's something you need to know."

"What?"

"Zo was in there when I left." My revelation was met with silence, but all the noise in the background let me know he hadn't hung up the phone.

"Cliff?"

"I'm here."

"Did you hear what I said?"

"Yeah, but I'll wait for you to get here and explain," he replied before hanging up.

I knew I didn't have nearly as much time really needed to formulate the right words once I got to Cliff. Because of all the latest events that had taken place, I was having trouble thinking. Lorenzo may have been a lot of things and Lord knows they all weren't good, but he was still my son. *Was this God's sick, twisted sense of humor for the way I'd treated Zo, wishing him back out of my life recently? Was this gonna be my punishment, a lifetime of guilt for threatening to kill my only son?* I couldn't answer any of these questions until I found out whether or not he was still inside the building when it burned down. And even then I still wouldn't have the answers.

"What did the office want?" I asked Melissa once her call had ended.

"They were watching the news and they said three of our girls were supposed to work tonight; none of them are answering their phone."

"Keep trying to reach them. We gotta go."

68

Within five minutes we were out the door heading towards the mysterious devastation we anticipated.

I drove from memory because my mind was being pulled in more directions than God ever intended it to be. So much shit had gone wrong in the last few days, to say it was all just bad luck would be making an understatement. I found myself asking whose life this was because there was no way this was Shayna Blizzard's story! Pulling in the parking lot amongst the cops, firemen, meat wagon and news crew meant things weren't going to get any better either.

I didn't proceed to get out until I saw Cliff, but he waved me back in, and hopped in the backseat.

"Start talking," he ordered.

"I got a call that Zo was down here and he'd been locked in the office with some chick for a day and a half."

"How long ago did all this happen?" he asked.

"A little over an hour ago, I guess."

"Okay, so what did you do?"

"I came down here and told him to get his shit together and get the fuck out."

"What exactly was he doing when you got here?"

"Is this for you or your police report?" I asked, suspiciously.

"If it was for my report your ass would be downtown."

"Fuck you mean?" I asked, looking at him in the rearview mirror.

"We'll get to that, just answer my questions, please."

"Whatever. When I got here, him and the bitch was in the office high out they mind, fuckin'."

"Who was the girl?"

"Trish."

"I thought she was Alicia's friend?"

"Cliff, what the fuck does that matter?" I asked irritated.

He had the good sense not to say anything smart, but instead, waited on me to continue.

"Anyway, I told him to clean up his mess, and if he couldn't lay low from now on, then he needed to get the fuck out of DC, period."

"Was he listening?"

"Does he ever listen?"

"What about the girl, what did you do with her?"

For the obvious reason I didn't like that question, even if it was coming from him. This was my time to see what he knew though because fire wouldn't cover up bullet holes.

"I didn't do shit with her except fire her trifling ass," I replied.

"You fired her?"

"Come on, slim, you know the rules just as well as everybody on my payroll. We don't do drugs, and we don't mix business with pleasure."

"Is that why you two look like you just rolled out of bed?" Cliff asked, sarcastically.

"Man fuck you! Matter fact, get out my goddamn truck with that bullshit!"

"You're right, that was uncalled for, I'm sorry."

"I ain't tryna hear that shit. I gotta go so you need to step out of my ride."

"You can't go nowhere just yet," he said, slowly.

"And why the fuck not?"

"Because the cops wanna ask you some questions."

"You are a cop negro!"

"Nah, I mean some official police business-type shit."

"For what?"

"Because the cameras at the end of the alley saw you come in and leave, and not too long after that, the building exploded. Think like a white person for a second, no offense Melissa," he said, turning his attention toward her briefly. The look on his face said he was serious but also sincere.

"None taken," she replied, sarcastically. Melissa had been listening to the two of them go and back and forth without saying a word. Up until now, she had never thought Cliff to be the type of friend/ex to turn on Shay. But, honestly, the more he talked, and the way he was questioning her, caused Melissa the uncertainty of his true intentions.

"Hold up, I own this club so why should my coming here be viewed as suspicious?"

"It shouldn't be, but at the same time, nobody else came or went before or after the fire, so that makes the list of suspects short for the moment. It's better to get your name cleared now to avoid anyone wanting to dig further into your life. We both know how that could turn out."

I knew he was right, but my distrust for what society considered law and order was real. As it was, it seemed like the whole U.S. of A was on the verge of exploding, due to all the racial tension, and mistreatment by white America against minorities —white cops killing young black men with an alarming frequency, and I'm supposed to trust those same mufuckas to look at me and not be suspicious?

Shit, from day one, a white man ain't never looked at a black woman with more than lust in his eyes. Not to mention, running my enterprise the way I do, and in the city I do it in, gives me a good look at corruption up close. When it came to fuckin' people over, the government was 'bout that life! Even knowing this though, I still knew a conversation now, was better than one later. I just had to ask myself how far under the microscope I wanted to be?

"Melissa, wait here," I said opening my door, waiting for Cliff to lead the way.

"Don't worry, I'll be with you the whole time," he said, taking my arm.

We were headed towards the front of the building, but we hadn't taken more than five steps when I saw a face coming towards me that shouldn't have been.

"What the fuck?" I mumbled under my breath, as Raheem stopped in front of us.

"Are you okay?" he asked, searching my face, intensely.

"She's fine," Cliff said, holding onto me, protectively.

"What are you doing here?" I managed to ask emotionlessly.

"I saw the fire on the news and I was worried."

"How did you know it was my club?" I asked.

"Just because I haven't been around you doesn't mean I haven't kept tabs on you, sweetheart."

"Don't. Don't call me pet names and act like you give a fuck!"

"Maybe you should leave," Cliff suggested, taking a step towards Rah. I didn't need the drama of physical violence right now, but part of me wanted to punch Rah my damn self, so it was hard to tell Cliff not to.

"Is that what you want?" Rah asked me.

My mind was saying 'hell yeah', and I couldn't get the words out quickly enough. But, when I opened my mouth to speak wouldn't shit come out. Again, it infuriated me that this mufucka still affected me the way he did, but I didn't know how to stop it.

"Ms. Blizzard?" a heavy set white man said, interrupting my already scattered thoughts.

"Yes?"

"I'm Detective Grobich, DC P.D homicide, and I need to ask you a few questions."

"Homicide?" I heard my voice echo, and although my eyes were on him, my focus remained on the word 'homicide'.

"Yes, ma'am. We don't think the explosion or subsequent fire was an accident," he replied.

"I see. What do you need to ask me?"

"Tell me exactly what you were doing here an hour ago?" he asked, bluntly.

"I just came to check on things. I tend to do that while the club is closed to the public," I answered, somewhat truthfully.

"And exactly what part of the club did you go in?"

Immediately, the question sent off warning bells in my brain. But, not answering didn't seem to be an option, especially if I didn't want to arouse suspicion.

"My private elevator takes me straight into my office," I replied.

"Did you go anywhere else?" he asked.

"No."

"Was anyone in the office with you?" he asked.

"No."

"Exactly, who else would have access to your private office?"

"Why?" I asked.

"I'm just wondering, ma'am," he replied politely.

"Well, the day to day management staff. It's not like we keep it locked up tight because my vault is top of the line."

"Okay. And no one was in there with you at any time?"

"I already answered that."

"Where did you go when you left here?

"To my Mom's house."

"And she can corroborate that?"

"I can," Raheem interjected.

"And who are you, sir?"

"A family friend, Raheem Miles."

"How long did Mrs. Blizzard stay?"

"About twenty minutes," Rah answered.

"Where did you go from there, Ms. Blizzard?"

"I went home," I replied. I stared at Rah longer than I had anticipated and wondered what he was thinking.

I probably looked crazy to him sitting in front of my own Mother's house, especially since he knew he was the reason I hadn't gone in.

"Do you know why anyone would target your establishment Mrs. Blizzard?" Detective Grobich asked.

"No."

"How many enemies do you have?"

His question caught me off guard. He didn't ask me *if* I had any enemies, but *how many* I had. I studied him closer for a moment, taking in his sloppiness that was barely concealed in his cheap suit. The puffy cheeks and red eyes hinted at drinking, while the stains on his teeth made me question the police department's benefit's package. Was it possible for the low level nobody to know who I was? Maybe. Or, maybe he was simply making assumptions because I was a woman with a legitimate sex business.

"I don't have any enemies," I replied, neutrally.

"Because you do such good business?" he asked, with what looked like a devious smirk on his face.

"Because," I paused, "it's not good business to have ene-mies," I stated truthfully, and in a more professional tone. "An enemy's sole purpose is to find a way to eliminate or destroy you. Why should I wait for that to happen?"

"So, you take a proactive approach and eliminate your enemies?" he asked carefully.

"Is that what you heard me say?"

"Is that what I should've heard?"

"Are you two gonna dance all day?" Raheem asked.

74

"I can go as long as she can."

"Or, you could talk to my lawyer," I said, reminding him that this entire conversation was a privilege.

"Mrs. Blizzard do you know of all the employees who were in the building when you came in?"

"No, but I know three of my girls were scheduled for today and they haven't been answering their phones. And my head of security, Leroy Joes, was there."

"What are the women's names?"

"I'll have to get them for you."

"Well, so far, the fire department has found six bodies. Two of which, were in your office and are believed to have gunshot wounds. Know anything about that?"

My mind started racing. There shouldn't have been two people still in my office, let alone both of them be shot.

"Shot?" I managed to mumble.

"Yes, ma'am, executed."

"Wer-were they women?" I asked, fearfully. I knew I wouldn't like the answer either way.

"One woman, one man."

All I kept hearing was the resounding echo, 'one man', bouncing around my brain, and then my knees buckled. Luckily for me I had the good grace to be unconscious before I hit the floor.

When I came to I found myself in my own bed. I almost believe everything had been a dream until I noticed I was still dressed in the sweat suit I'd thrown on this morning. It was mind blowing to know I'd really fucking fainted. Knowing with almost absolute certainty my son was the yet unidentified second body, was a damn good reason to hit the deck though.

Internally, I knew it was gonna take a while to comprehend given the fact that our relationship was 'complicated', to say the least. *How would I grieve for a son I never really knew? Did all the secrets and demons die with him? Would it somehow be easier to heal now?* I didn't have the answer to any of those questions, but I knew they wouldn't simply go away.

Right now, the smell of smoke was a welcome distraction. Thankfully, it was the smoke of some good green instead of the smoke coming from a building with burning bodies in it. Whoever it was blowin' wasn't in the bedroom with me, so I had to do like Toucan Sam and follow my nose.

My body groaned in protest, a little, but eventually, I managed to roll out of bed and make my way to the living room. When I finally made it to the living room the sight before me almost caused me to attack the floor like I'd done earlier.

"What the fuck are you doing?" I asked.

"Uh, watching The Purge: Election Year, and smoking a blunt."

"I mean, what the fuck are you doing in my house, Raheem!"

"Chill, Shay, I was just sitting here until you woke up, so I would know you a'ight."

"Oh, so now you give a damn about my welfare? Boy, bye! Get out my damn house with all that."

"Yo', will you just calm the fuck down! You've been through a lot."

"Yeah, I know, and most of it's because of you!"

"Well, I'm sorry!" he yelled, jumping up in my face.

I wanted to knock his mufuckin' head off, but the truth was, his words had me paralyzed. He'd never apologized before.

"You-you're what?" I asked, wondering if he'd say it again.

"I'm sorry, Shay. I've wanted to tell you that for years, but you never wanted to hear me out I know what I did was fucked up and I know I hurt you, but I swear to you I've been living with that pain too."

"Rah-."

"Just listen for a second, please. You were right. I should've at least been man enough to have that conversation with you about kids. I was immature. I won't make any other excuses. I swear to you I regret the pain I continue to cause you, but I don't want you to think I got off scot-free."

"Wh-what do you mean?"

"You know about the eighty-twenty rule. I had to learn it the hard way and it came with an incredible loss. I know what it feels like to lose a child," he whispered, stepping closer to me and gently caressing my cheek with his hand.

I could see the pain in his eyes and its depth seemed bottomless. I didn't even know I was crying until I felt him wipe away my tears. I didn't wanna be vulnerable in front of him, but I felt the floodgates of all my suppressed emotions start to crumble.

"I don't know what to say," I whispered.

He didn't want my words though, and I was instantly lost the moment his lips touched mine.

Aryanna

A Savage Love 2

CHAPTER NINE

MISUNDERSTOOD

Who can see the tears I can't see? Which of you knows my head or heart enough to start piecing together the real me few have seen? I can't deny the truthful lies that my eyes project to protect the secrets my soul hides, but I confess half-truths are still lies.

So, who am I? It's not like you care because I'm aware that you see me only in terms of what you think you know. You're not beholden to the truth, in fact, you prefer to use misdirection and tactics of deflection to see me only in terms of, what's in darkness comes to light, eventually.

The difference between you and I is, my possession of clarity for the make-up that is mine. I understand me deeply, embracing the organized noise that defines chaos in a way that places the less enlightened beneath me. Not speaking from a narcissistic point of view, only seeking to show and prove the advantages of accepting the darkest sides of you, me, or anybody really.

Facing the devil in me allows me to conclude that you can't really know me because you don't know you yet. Who are you?

Have you met the multitudes of people shaping your character, or have years of food for thought been last in the air, occupying space between your ears? You don't hear me though, just like you don't know what scars reality has burned into this woman you think you know. Yet, you claim to understand. You claim to be a fan of the changes made and the work I've done, all the while not knowing one real thing about who I am.

It's sad, but it's good. Why? Because only I can see the advantages of being 'Misunderstood' from the inside.

Dear Jr,

I can't tell you how great it was to spend time with you, it's been way too long since we did that. Things change every day and I hardly notice, but you staying the same in terms of your love and loyalty mean the world to me. I'm blessed; that's how you make me feel. I wish we didn't live so far apart because I could seriously get used to seeing you all the time, but I guess the time for that will come right?

Since we've last spoken I've given considerable thought to your surprise for me. I know my initial reaction wasn't what you'd hoped for or expected, but I'm sure you can understand. Just like I understand you only wanting to make me happy.

You're the only man in my life, other than my father, who truly wanted to do that. So, please, understand that such a grand gesture caught me off guard. I love it though! I absolutely love it and all the thought you put into making it happen. I just wanna say thank you, sweetheart. It's crazy how I never told you what I wanted, but somehow knew what it would take to complete me. I guess we really are one in the same. Lol!

Anyways, I just wanted to clear that up with you because I felt like I came off as being ungrateful for you and all that you are. I love you more than anything or anyone in the world. I'll see you soon!

Love always, M.

CHAPTER TEN

I wanted to pull back from the kiss and run as fast as I could in the opposite direction, but I felt my body molding to his like old times. A kiss was never just a kiss with him, it was communication that required no words. The magic in this man's tongue could have a mute speaking fluently. I could hear screaming far off in the corners of my mind because things never ended with a kiss like this.

Nah, this mufucka was declaring war. And with this realization came the thundering of my heart as I felt his fingers on my clit. I don't know when his hands journeyed into my pants, but I was surely gonna come unglued if we didn't stop now.

"Rah, wait. We-we can- can't," I painted into his open mouth, even as my tongue continued to seek his.

"I know, baby," he whispered, pulling me closer to him.

"Rah. . .," I moaned, when his finger slipped in between my pussy lips, and dove inside me.

The melody he'd been playing was so sweet and familiar, I felt the tears building just as fast as my climax was. Now the screaming in my head was louder than a tornado warning, and just when I thought I had one more shot to stop this from happening, I made the fatal mistake of looking him in the eyes. A storm of need and desperation swirled with a hurricane's intensity, flooding my mind with times past when we used to dance like this.

I'd lost myself once with this man and I knew the danger of that mistake, but looking into eyes that I knew mirrored my own, showed me the truth. I was already lost again.

"You win," I sighed, finally letting my arms wrap themselves around him so I could feel his muscles ripple.

Before I knew what was happening, he'd literally thrown me on the couch, but I remembered this too from our past. I had barely rolled over in the face-down, ass-up position he liked, when I felt my sweat pants being yanked down, and my ass cheeks being spread.

The minute his tongue glided across my asshole, I came hard enough to make my knees wobble. I didn't have to say it out loud because my body knew daddy was home.

I felt his finger in my ass, and then he was sucking on my pussy like it contained the last traces of oxygen in the world. I don't remember when my arms gave out, but by the time I felt him tickling my sweet spot with the head of his dick, I was literally face-down, praying my neck didn't break.

"Rah you need a-a-um-con-."

But it was too late because he'd slammed that good dick home, and I wasn't about to give it back. His chants of *'oh shit'*, as my pussy muscles imprisoned him, motivated me. Every time he dove inside me I threw that ass back, and the fight was on. I came twice before I felt the heat of his climax race to its destination, but I knew his body just like he knew mine.

"Hold on," I told him getting up. Going to my C.D. player I selected what we needed for the occasion, knowing he would appreciate the trip down memory lane.

As soon as James Brown started singing about this being a man's world, I stripped off my clothes and stood before him with the gleam of defiance in my eyes. We had battled to this song on many occasions because according to the lyrics, *'this is a man's world, but it wouldn't be nothing without a woman or a girl'*.

"Fuck me like you missed me," I ordered, pushing him down on the couch.

For the next three hours we put every square foot of my place to good use. Every surface was touched, and I had him inside every hole on me that he could fit, until we reached mutual surrender on the kitchen floor.

"Amazing," he painted, reaching for me.

I understood what I'd just shared with him, but the intimacy of cuddling was just too much right now. I dodged his embrace by getting up to get a blunt to smoke, hopping I could stop the movie of memories I was still seeing. No one in their right mind would regret mind-blowing, toe-popping, I love you, long time, sex. But I wasn't in my right mind at the moment. Raheem was dangerous to me. He was worse than heroin and PCP combined, and I was a true junky for what he had.

"Fuck," I mumbled in frustration. I lit a blunt and turned the music off, before sitting on the couch.

"Shayna-."

"Don't. Don't say shit because this changes nothing."

"This changes everything and you know it," he said, coming to stand in front of me. I did know it, but part of me was hoping denial could make it less true.

"Look, man, I'm dealing with a lot right now and I can't handle no more. I appreciate the sex, but it doesn't gotta be no more than that."

"Who you lying to, Slim? Me or you?"

"What?"

"Listen, I get that you're dealing with a lot, but don't you think you could use someone to talk to?"

"Yeah, but I'd prefer that person to be someone I can trust. Know anyone?"

Looking up at him I could tell he didn't like my comment, but instead of saying some slick shit back, he sat next to me. I did my best to ignore his presence, but him being that close and that naked, had my body saying *'bitch get some'!*

I wanted to believe he really was sorry, and he had been miserable without me, but I'd heard all the best lines before. By the code of the streets I was a pimp, so how could I fall for another nigga's game? *Because the heart wants what the heart wants,* a little voice in my head echoed. That shit worked out good in chick flicks, but this was real life, and a bitch had to guard her heart closer than her money.

"I meant what I said Shayna. I'm sorry. I know it's easy to sit back now and see where I fucked up, but that don't make me any less apologetic. After doing that bid, all I wanted was to come home to you.

Then I came out and got caught up in all the things I'd missed out on. I lost sight of what was important, Bae. I didn't plan to have a baby with Rosalyn, but when she told me she was pregnant I felt a love I'd never known. It's crazy because even after I left I couldn't stop thinking about you."

"Yeah, whatever nigga."

"It's true. I even named my daughter Kashay."

"You did what?" I asked, not believing that any woman was gonna go for their daughter being partially named after another woman.

The sad smile he gave me made me believe he might not be so full of shit.

"Yeah, I called her Shay-shay. She was truly a daddy's girl."

"What happened?" I asked once he had gone silent.

I could feel the hurt radiating from his body and it made me want to reach out to him. The way he wore his obvious hurt made me think about Zo and my own inability to feel that way. A child never asks to be born, and in truth, I'd taken that out on Zo his entire life. Not because I didn't love him, but because I never saw myself as a mother.

I'd had him during what I considered my prime and I just couldn't see giving up my lifestyle, or the way I made money. Did that make me a bad person? Absolutely! But by the time I realized it, the guilt was too heavy for me to carry. So, I left it where it lay. Somehow I didn't think it was gonna be that easy this time.

"Shay was like any other kid. Fun, loving, full of life and adventure, but sometimes that adventure didn't know its limits. When I left DC I didn't go far. I got a little house out in Maryland, figuring it would be better to raise a child away from the city. I was wrong. m-m-my baby was taken right from in front of our house."

The break in his voice tugged at my heart hard, but I didn't know how to respond to the words he'd spoken. Saying I was sorry seemed like I would be spitting in his face. All I could think to do was pass him the blunt and hopefully release his mind from the demons that haunted him. We sat in silence until the blunt was gone, but by then, I'd rolled another one so we just kept blowin'.

"How much do you remember about my son? I asked.

"I remember everything you told me."

"Oh. Well, a few days ago he came back to town. To say I was against the move is an understatement, especially now. Ironically, shortly after he'd showed up, his baby's mama ends up dead. I wanted him to leave, to just disappear and stay gone. But I didn't want him to die."

"What makes you think he's dead?" Rah asked.

"Because. I lied to the police, when I left the club my son and one of my workers were in my office."

"That explains the fainting. When I asked Melissa about it, all she had to say was it had something to do with your son. I assumed he was in the building, but for your sake I hoped I was wrong."

"I'm not even sure how to feel or how to grieve. I mean, I just feel numb right now, you know?"

"Yeah, I do know. Everybody grieves in their own way though, sweetheart, you just can't be afraid to go through the process."

I didn't know what the process consisted of, but I wasn't looking forward to having a major meltdown. I'm not too tough to cry, I just don't see the point in it.

"I know you, Shayna, and you're gonna fight anything you see as weakness in yourself. Mourning you son ain't weak though."

I took his hand when he offered it, but I didn't lean on him when he tried to pull me towards him.

"Listen, it's been a long day and until we know something for sure, we should put this conversation on hold," he suggested, gathering his clothes and putting them on.

As much as I hated to admit it, I knew he was right, but that's not something I was prepared to concede to his ass.

"What you wanna eat?"

"Huh?"

"You didn't think I was just gonna leave you in your time of need did you? Girl, please. I know how stubborn you are, and you'll never admit when you need help. I'm here though, and I know you need to eat, so what's it going to be?"

I hid my smile behind a cloud of smoke, not wanting to encourage him in any way. I could lie to him, but I couldn't lie to myself, because I did miss the way he used to pamper me; I had trained him well.

"I'm in the mood for something Italian," I replied.

"I can get behind that, is there anything else you need while I'm out?"

"Nah, I'm good."

"A'ight, I'll be back," he said, heading for the front door.

I couldn't deny the feelings swirling within me, but I knew I had to be careful, because falling in love with this nigga wasn't an option. I didn't have room in my life for dudes and their distractions. Rah could serve a purpose as long as it suited me, but love didn't have shit to do with it.

Once I was nice and tight, I put the rest of the blunt in the ashtray and went to the bedroom in search of my phone. My first call had to be to my girl so she'd know I was a'ight.

"What's up, bitch?" I said, when she answered.

"What's up, boo, how you holding up?"

"I'm maintaining, I guess. This last week has been so crazy, it feels surreal."

"I hear you. You ain't mad at me are you?"

"Why you ask me that?"

"For letting Raheem take you back to your house," she replied, hesitantly.

"I assume you had a good reason."

"I did. After you had your episode I went back to the office, figuring I could help locate our girls, or at least, their families."

"Okay, first of all, I didn't have no damn episode, my blood sugar was low. More importantly, did you find our girls?"

"Sadly no, which means we've lost five girls in under a week. I knew you'd want to call a meeting on that alone, so I set it up with all of your employees for tomorrow at ten a.m."

"Okay. What did the cops say?"

"Nothing to me directly, but I know the body count was eight in total, and of course the club is still closed."

"A'ight, I'll get in touch with Cliff about the investigation. I'll meet you in the office at 9 a.m."

"A'ight, girl, try not to hurt yourself tonight."

"Fuck you talking 'bout, bitch?"

"Come on, I've known you too long not to know when you've been thoroughly fucked," she replied.

"And on that note, I gotta go. I'll see you in the morning," I said, ending the call before she could get any further into my business.

I thought about calling Cliff, but that conversation could wait until tomorrow. I decided a stiff drink was in order, and no sooner had the ice cubes hit my glass, I heard my door opening.

"So you just took my keys without permission?" I asked Rah.

"Seemed like the smart thing to do since I knew you wouldn't be putting any clothes on," he replied, smiling.

I couldn't argue with his logic, or the dance my stomach was doing from the smell of the food. I met him in the living room where he'd laid out the spread on the coffee table. It was something like old times, and not as awkward as I thought it would be.

The conversation wasn't forced and it was actually good not to be alone, or entertaining some random nigga. Still, I didn't want him to get too comfortable.

"You know you ain't spending the night, right?" I asked.

"Oh, yeah? You got somebody coming over to take my place?"

"And if I do, so-," before I could finish my slick come-back, my phone started ringing. My clock read 1:43 a.m. which meant the call was more than likely, more bad news. I took a deep breath, squared my shoulders, and answered.

"Hello."

"Is it him," Raheem asked, puzzled.

"Cliff?"

"It's not him Shayna, it's not Zo!"

It took a minute for his words to register, but when they did, I still had one question.

"If it's not him then where the hell is our son Cliff? Where's Lorenzo?"

CHAPTER ELEVEN

For the next week that same question continued to roll around my mind. There had been no word or sighting of Zo, by me, or any of my people, not even at the memorial service held in part for Alicia. It was like the nigga had just vanished.

By the end of the first week I was asking myself if maybe Zo had caused the explosion out of spite or revenge. The more I thought about it the madder I got. *Fucking with my money like that, not to mention all the heat it put on my business.* Shit had me wishing I could wrap my hands around his neck. At the same time having him out of sight and away from me, seemed like an even trade, especially since I didn't have to carry the guilt of his death. There were a lot of issues Lorenzo and I had to eventually work through, but right now all that seemed like tomorrows problems.

At least, those had been my initial thoughts. Then, the second week after the fire Cliff informed me that not only had Zo been spotted in the club that day, but his prints had also been found in Alicia's house.

Like I'd said, the cops in DC have long memories, and now my son was public enemy number one on everybody's radar, for a total of nine bodies.

Despite what the news said, they weren't trying to talk to him, they were gonna bury his black ass whenever they caught up to him. Shit was so real, I was held up in my own house, turning it into my base of operations to avoid scrutiny on my company! There weren't enough fleas on Fluffy to make me walk away from all the money I was making, and the quiet empire I'd built. A bitch had to be smart though.

Luckily for me, I had a right-hand like Melissa, someone supremely efficient in getting shit done without having to be told twice. Sometimes, she knew what to get done without even being told. Plus, the more I kept her around, the less likely I was to let Raheem fall back into my bed. I hadn't lied when I told him he couldn't spend the night, but he'd just barely beat the sun.

I can't lie, the dick wasn't just good, the nigga's shit was gold! Still, I'd somehow managed to avoid him for two weeks while I refocused on my business, and getting back to the money. I didn't know how long it was gonna last, especially since I knew he was still in town. I thought he might've been taking care of my mother just to get into my good graces, but now I was thinking he genuinely cared.

***

"Did you hear me?" Melissa asked, snapping her fingers in my face.

"Huh?" I replied.

"Bitch, I've been talking to you for the last five minutes. Where the fuck you been?"

"My bad. You know I've got a lot on my mind."

"A'ight, well, we can take a break," she said, sitting on the couch next to me.

It was just 8 p.m., but it felt like I'd been up for three days straight without sleep. Shit always got hectic around import/export time in this business because my records had to be meticulous.

"You hungry?" she asked.

"You cooking?" I countered. We both laughed at that because we already knew the girl would burn water. I wouldn't let her in my kitchen even if it was to fix my last meal.

"You funny, Slim, but you know I can order take-out like a mufucka."

"True shit. What are you gonna order?"

"I'm feeling like some Chinese food. You with that?"

"Does it come with a happy ending?" I asked, pinching her nipple through the tan top she was wearing.

"You keep playing and the happy ending is gonna come before the food gets here," she warned.

"Nope, feed me first, bitch," I said, getting up and going to the bathroom. Looking at myself in the mirror, I noticed new lines that I hadn't seen before. Black don't crack, so me having lines and shit meant I was stressing, entirely, too much.

"I need a vacation," I said to myself, washing my hands before going back to the living room.

Just as I about to sit down, there was a knock at my door.

"Damn, that was fast," I said to Melissa, assuming it could only be the food since mufuckas knew not to show up to my spot unannounced— that was the quickest way to get your feelings hurt.

Even knowing this, my first mistake was not bothering to look through the peep hole or ask who it was. Unfortunately, I didn't realize my error until I'd snatched the door open and came face to face with Raheem.

"You know better," I told him, hoping he couldn't hear how hard my heart was beating.

"Yeah, I do, but I wanted to see you. Plus, I come with a peace offering."

I could smell the beef and broccoli through the bag, but I also thought I smelled a rat.

"Melissa?" I said, turning to face her.

"'Sup?"

"Did you by chance call Raheem instead of the Chinese place, with your meddling ass?"

"No, why?" I simply stepped aside so she could see him at the door, along with the bag of take out in his hand. I was tempted to lay into her ass for being messy, and all up in my business. But, at the sight of him, I knew the look of disappointment on her face was real.

"Shay, she didn't call me. I just know you haven't been getting out much, and I remembered how much you love the Chinese food from Lucy's in southeast."

"You went way out there to get me some food?" I asked.

"Beef and broccoli, double cooked pork, and egg rolls of course," he replied, walking in and sitting the bag on my coffee table.

"We're working," Melissa said.

"And we already ordered food," I stated.

"Ah, but this ain't just food, Slim, this is Lucy's," he stated, already pulling containers out of the bag, causing my mouth to water. I was already being pulled by my nose, as I closed the door and made a beeline for the kitchen to grab some plates.

"Really?" Melissa whispered, coming up behind me.

"What? It's just a meal, and I never said you had to leave," I whispered right back.

"Well, I'm not leaving because we've got work to do!"

"Fine."

I took the plates to Rah and he dished the food out, even making a plate for Melissa. If it's one thing I'm not shy about, besides my sexual appetite, it's my food intake; when good food is around there ain't no time for games, and that was my attitude as I dug into my plate like a fat girl on a mission.

For ten straight minutes there wasn't a word spoken. We were all content letting Lucy's speak for us. I had just grabbed my second egg roll when there came another knock at the door. Nobody moved to answer it until I gave Melissa a look.

"What?" she asked.

"It's your order, Slim," I told her, reaching for the sweet and sour sauce.

"Ugh!" came her reply, as she got up and went to take care of the delivery man.

"When was the last time you ate Shay?" Rah asked.

"I don't even know. I been so busy and stressed that I been on a steady diet of weed and junk food."

"You know better. You gonna fuck around and lose them curves," he replied, smiling.

"Negro, please. You know I'ma be juicy for life!"

"That's for damn sure!" Melissa said, rejoining us, and sitting more food on the table.

"What did you get?" I asked.

"Boneless ribs, shrimp fried rice, and more egg rolls."

"Hell, yeah!" I said, making room on my plate for the additions.

"I'm surprised you ain't got the game on," Rah commented, looking at the sixty inch taking up my wall.

"What game?" I asked.

"We've got work to do," Melissa interjected.

"The Land and Dub City," Rah replied, reaching for the remote, simultaneously ignoring Melissa's protests.

"I didn't even know they were playing tonight! We're still gonna get our work done, boo, don't trip," I told her, already locked in on the screen.

We managed to get through the rest of the first half, watching Lebron and Kyrie do battle with the super team led by the Splash Brothers and Slim Reaper, Mr. Kevin Durant himself.

I'm a huge KD fan because he's from the city, even though I felt some type of way about him not wanting to play for Washington this year. I wouldn't let his business affect my personal views on him though. I mean, I knew all too well the slums in which he'd come from. You had to respect what he'd turned into now, and they were putting on one helluva show down in Cleveland right now.

I wanted to kick back with the leftover Chinese food, a couple blunts, and a few shots of dark liquor to finish the game, but as soon as half time hit, Melissa was on my ass. I'd gotten so caught up talking shit with Rah about his Cleveland Cavaliers that I damn near forgot homegirl was in the room. Basketball was just one of the many things me and this nigga had in common, and we loved going to the games together.

I use to love how he always played with my pussy at some point during the game, mixing my screams of fulfillment with those of diehard fans. Looking at him now as he sat on my loveseat, I could tell we were both remembering the same thing, and I could feel that thumping starting in my panties again.

"Come on, bitch, let's get this work done," I said, switching my attention, in hopes of quieting the hunger that was building.

I managed to ignore his laughs with a straight face as we got back to the paperwork. The sex industry was a multi-billion-dollar business, and it wasn't just retained to the good old U.S.A. I did business all around the globe, and every month I did some imports and exports. Right now, I had three girls going to Saudi Arabia for a total of fifteen million dollars, and I was getting paid just to babysit the more four girls I had coming in from South Korea.

I never forced my girls to go anywhere, and I didn't deal with women who had been forced into this way of life. The price for babysitting depended on how long I was asked to do so. If anything seemed funny about the money, then I acquired the assets in question.

I believed in getting money in every way when it came to this lifestyle. Even though we were up in my penthouse handling million dollar deals, I'd just hired two white girls who were sisters named Kim and Sherri who'd been working the track sucking dick at forty dollars a blow. They weren't high class hoes or even D-league material, just some regular hoes from Knoxville, Tennessee who needed a job, and well, I considered myself an equal opportunity employer.

"You got all the paperwork for the Korean chicks?" I asked Melissa.

"It'll be ready before they get here next week."

"Cool, what's the projected start date for building a new club?"

"Well, the police haven't finished their investigation, and word is we're looking at another couple of weeks, at least," she replied, hesitantly.

"That's bullshit! See, now they fuckin' with my money."

"Why not have Cliff intervene?" Rah asked.

"If it were that easy don't you think we would've done that already?" Melissa asked, sarcastically.

"Besides, with our son's name all in the mix he can't go near the situation," I said.

"Okay, so build a new club somewhere else," he suggested.

"You got any prime real-estate you wanna offer up?" Melissa asked.

"Actually, I do."

"Say what? When did you become a business man?" I asked, skeptically.

"You gotta admit you were a great teacher of many things," he replied, licking his lips.

"Yeah, but we ain't talkin' about eating pussy," Melissa sneered.

"No, we're talking about selling it, and I learned the price of pussy at her feet," Rah said, giving Melissa a challenging look.

"Tell me about this property," I said.

"Well, I've got a few properties around the city and MD, but I'm thinking about one of my warehouses."

"A warehouse is only one level," I replied.

"True, but we knockin' that down and buildin' what we want. Plus, it takes up a whole city block."

"Do you know how long that'll take?" Melissa asked.

"I do, but if we're out to make money and eliminate competition, then it's go big or go home. In the meantime, I've got some connections and I can have your girls dancing tonight if you want."

"Oh, yeah? So what makes you think it's a good idea for us to go into business together?" I asked.

"Right," Melissa chimed in.

"One thing we can always agree on is money. We're both about that action like super heroes, but we can bring in a third party to make sure shit is smooth."

"And why would I trust someone who trusts you?" I asked.

"Because, I'm talking about your mom."

My mother knew what I was into, but I'd never actually had her all up in my business. It wasn't an idea that really appealed to me, but if anyone could keep this nigga honest it was Miss Ida Mae.

"So, you're connected in every major club all over the city? 'Cause Shayna's girls don't dance for EBT cards," Melissa said.

"You calling my bluff?" he asked her, but his eyes never left mine.

"You've been gone awhile, Rah. I don't think a little show and prove is too much to ask before you ask Shayna to trust you around the money."

"Right," I told him, in total agreement Melissa.

"Okay. Get dressed for a night out, Raheem demanded. Melissa, have ten of the best girls ready to shake their asses in an hour, and have the driver waiting for us out front with the car. Oh, and you should change too, that way you can get an up-close and personal look."

Melissa looked at me, seeking my approval and I gave her the nod.

"This is your one shot my nigga, don't fuck it up," I told him.

Aryanna

CHAPTER TWELVE

There was no way for me to know I might not have been ready for what I'd let Melissa talk us into, but when we pulled up at National Airport I felt the first twinges of nerves.

"Nah, Slim, you gotta let me prove myself," Rah said smiling, when I tried to question him.

When my girls got there we were escorted through the airport and through a private door that took us straight to the tarmac where a GIV awaited us. I wanted to ask whose plane we were boarding, but I was silenced with a look from Rah that told me I'd just have to embark on this adventure.

The party started as soon as we reached thirty thousand feet with bottles of Ciroc and Grey Goose making a heavy rotation. A 50 Cent classic, *Hustlaz Ambition*, was knocking through the speakers, and my girls were practicing their moves on the pole in the back of the plane. I warned them not to get too fucked up because they still had work to do, even though I had no idea exactly *where* they'd be doing it.

"You're full of surprises," I said to Rah, accepting the glass of Champagne he'd provided, as he took a seat next to me.

"Is that a bad thing? When was the last time a man was spontaneous with you?" he questioned.

"Don't try to get all up in my mix, Rah, and I never said surprises were a bad thing. It all depends on who's doing the surprising, and you know I don't trust your ass.

"Yeah, I do know that, but that's personal, and this is all about business."

"My money is always personal, Slim," I told him, sipping my drink.

His response was a chuckle as he stepped away to answer his phone. I had to admit, there was a certain thrill to just being whisked away off into the night somewhere. Even though they could afford it, none of the niggas I fucked with had ever done anything like this for me, but I was okay with that. You couldn't miss what you didn't have. Besides, I made damn sure I pampered myself with whatever I desired. I did miss the way Rah operated though— he'd always been my heart.

"My apologies, my business partner was just wondering what time we'd be arriving," Rah said, retaking his eat.

"Where are we going?"

"You just can't sit back and enjoy yourself, can you, Shay?"

"Like I said before, I don't trust your ass."

"Well, since I know that has very little to do with this adventure, let's speak on the issue. I'll never be able to change the past or the ways I've hurt you, Shayna. Just like I can't change all the magical moments we shared. At this point, we gotta take the good with the bad, but I think we can agree there was more good than bad."

"Speak for yourself."

"Okay fine, I know for me there was way more good than bad, and I know we can't get that back. What I am hoping we can do is build something new, and I'm willing to do that one brick at a time if necessary. I'm not asking you to trust me, I'm asking you to judge me on my actions in this moment, and each moment that follows. Can you do that?"

I contemplated his little speech while taking another swig of my Champagne. Matters of the heart could rarely be solved using the tools of logic. Love wasn't logical.

I didn't wanna believe I still loved this nigga in any way whatsoever, but there was something undeniable that wouldn't allow me to spit in his face and be done with him. I didn't trust him, and without that there was no way of building a relationship. So, if I couldn't build a relationship what did I have to lose? My heart was protected, my pussy was pleased, and there was a possibility I might be adding more capital to my empire.

"I'll try," I told him, extending my glass for a refill.

We sipped Champagne and enjoyed watching the entire game all over again while my girls partied in their own little world. At first Melissa seemed sullen, but now she was up shaking her ass too.

Before I knew it, the plane started its decent and we had to strap in for the touchdown. I still didn't know where we were, but it was good to be on the ground in one piece.

"Now what?" I asked, once we'd taxied to a stop.

"There's a Sprinter Van right outside to take us to the club," Rah replied.

"All this just to dance? You've done too much," Melissa said

"Let's see if you still feel that way in the morning," Rah replied, leading the way off the plane.

The first thing I noticed was the frigid air that smacked me in my face, damn near snatching my lungs out. A bitch could handle the winters in DC or even up top in New York, but this shit was too much! I opened my mouth to protest the fact out loud, and that's when I noticed something that made my stomach drop.

"Is this? This can't be what I think it is. . ."

"I'm afraid it is," Rah said, smiling.

"Nigga you brought me to Canada!" I exclaimed, in, both, disbelief and anger.

"Calm sown Shay-."

"Calm down? Mufucka, I'm in Canada! I understand you tryna make a point or prove your connections, but you gotta warn a bitch when she's leaving U.S. soil, fool-ass nigga!" I screamed as hard as the wind was blowing. I knew everything I was saying was probably coming across at a normal conversation level, but the look on my face should've been plain to read.

I mean, seriously, the U.S. was filled with strip clubs from coast to coast, so what the fuck was we doing in Canada?

"Shay, listen. Just calm down and relax," he said, taking my hand and leading me on the van. Once everybody was inside, we were off, and he was still holding my hand sitting next to me.

"Why Canada, Rah?" I asked.

"Well, I like their law better, for one. And, for two, the money is definitely better, but I'll let that speak for itself. You know as well as I do sex sells, and in foreign countries, especially, American girls can really make that money. I just wanted to show you what our neighbors next door had to offer before we go to Europe or Asia."

"I'm telling you now, Raheem, this shit better be worth my time," I warned.

"You with me now, and daddy's got you," he whispered into my ear, gently kissing my earlobe.

The shivers he sent up my spine lessened my apprehension a little, but when I looked at Melissa I found doubt swimming in her eyes. I tried giving her a reassuring smile, but her response was to stick her tongue out at me and roll up a blunt.

During the thirty-minute ride to the club Rah explained how he'd hooked up with some businessmen out of Montreal, and how they had turned him on to some up and coming clubs. Using what he'd learned from me, he'd talked his way into a few partnerships from here to Quebec, and he was touching some real paper up here in the north. His sales pitch to me was to have my girls dance up here, or ply their trade for twenty-five percent of the profits.

After discussing his list of clientele we came to a trial agreement. Now, the only thing left for me to do was go where the night took me.

I stepped into the club trying to take in the atmosphere as several sets of eyes turned my way. I knew mufuckas would drool over my black Versace bodysuit, and imagine all the things they could do to me with my gold Louis Vuitton red bottoms in the air.

My hair hung down perfectly. My jewelry was limited to a few gold bangles on each arm, and around my neck was a cross that fit nicely in between my firm titties. My walk was more of a glide that exuded sex and power, and I knew all too well the ability it had to captivate an entire room.

All eyes were on me, but *my* eyes were on the money. I was taking in the understated, yet, tasteful décor, as well as the number of girls dancing on the floor, and the stage set-up.

The place was crowded which was always a good thing, and I spotted just enough security to make sure it stayed a good thing for as long as the doors stayed open. There were beautiful women all around, but they hadn't seen nothing yet. Melissa came through the door behind me, rocking a fire red Versace body suit with matching stilettos. To look at her from the front in no way prepared you for all the ass she was carrying, and I heard the girl dancing closest to us say 'damn' when she got a peek at it.

My ten girls who were in identical black trench coats, followed us in with Raheem pulling up the rear. The party had officially arrived. I could hear Drake's *Hotline Bling* booming through the speakers, but a nod from Rah had Future encouraging everybody to *Fuck Up Some Commas*.

"Ladies, get my money," I told them.

One by one, they each came out of their jackets revealing bikinis and panty sets in a multitude of colors. Their physical beauty brought a hush over the crowd before the place erupted in thunderous applause that had all my girls showing their pearly white teeth.

"This is gonna be a good night," Rah said, taking my hand.

He led Melissa and I to an upstairs V.I.P. area where we got a private room, complete with cameras for us to watch the floor.

"What time does the club close?" Melissa asked.

"When the sun comes up," he replied, popping a bottle of Ace of Spades.

"So, we're gonna be here all night?" she asked.

"Don't worry, we'll just throw a private party," he replied, smiling.

"Stop grinning like that, nigga, 'cause ain't no way yo' dick gonna end up in her unless you want to lose it, feel me?" I said, smiling sweetly.

"That goes without saying, sweetheart," he said, passing us each a glasse of Champagne.

Sipping the cool liquid, I wondered what he had up his sleeve and how real shit was gonna get. I didn't have to wait long to find out though.

"You wanna fire this up?" he asked me.

"Is that a dipper?"

"And you know this." I read the look of fear in Melissa's eyes, clearly.

The dipper wasn't no joke, it was a combination of PCP and steroids soaked into a cigarette, and it could have you outside your mind. I'd only experienced the high one time, and that had been in my younger years; and the fact that I was even considering it now was a testament to how stressed I really was.

"You know we don't fuck with drugs, only bud," Melissa said.

Rah kept looking at me with his hand extended, but after I didn't reach for it, he lit it himself. The smell of it was a punch to my memory because it always smelled like finger nail polish remover. I continued sipping my drink, knowing it would only take moments for the high to kick in, and wondered how he would act. A lot of people went bat-shit crazy off the big dipper, pushing even the mild-mannered type off the deep end.

"You a'ight?" I asked him, warily.

"Yeah, I'm good, Slim. I'm hearing colors, but I'm good."

"This mufucka lunchin'," Melissa said, lighting a blunt to mask the smell of the dipper. The weed wouldn't cover it up, but I did love how the two blended together.

"Melissa, you gonna hit it?" I asked.

"Hell, nah."

"Good, make sure shit don't get too out of hand," I advised. Before she could read my intentions, I'd taken the dipper from Rah and hit it hard. I didn't even exhale the smoke before I hit it again, figuring two good tokes would put me where I wanted to be.

Melissa just shook her head as I passed it back to Rah and then took the blunt from her. I had just enough time to hit the blunt a good three times before the world changed, and I understood exactly what Rah meant about hearing colors. Time took on a life of its own and it seemed to go from a slow to hyper speed without warning. I saw myself set this blunt down like I was having an out of body experience. The next thing I knew, I was pulling Melissa onto my lap, and pulling her top down so I could suck her titties.

The feeling of her nipples in my mouth was beyond description, but she tasted so good I had to have all of her. Time slipped, and before I knew it we were in the sixty-nine position, and her cum tasted better than all the Champagne in the world. I drank it greedily, wanting more, and praying she never stopped convulsing over me. When I came my world shattered, and I lost my foothold on reality and space, but the moment Rah penetrated me, I was home again.

Somewhere in the mist, Melissa had switched positions, and now she was riding my face while I sucked her clit. I could feel my pussy thumping with need as Rah pounded my asshole, but the climax that was coming was worth the wait. This time when I came, I thought I would surely die because absolutely nothing in this world could feel as good as I was feeling.

Before I knew it, I was face down in Melissa's treasures, licking her ass while Raheem fed me death blows in the form of back shots. Every time he dove deep he gave me life, and, I, in turn, passed that gift along to Melissa through my tongue.

The rest of the night unfolded in a kaleidoscope of erotic images. I had gotten eaten multiple times, and I ate his dick up until his knees buckled. Melissa was always in the mix, but Rah never put his dick anywhere near her, so the party stayed friendly.

When the club shut down, I was exhausted, and coming down off a monster high, but I was more relaxed than I'd been in weeks. Melissa and I were laid up on the couch together in each other's arms while Rah went to check on business.

"Helluva night," I said, stroking her hair gently.

"'Bout dat life is all I can say," she replied, playing with my nipple.

"I've known you for a while Melissa, and we've been in business just as long. What do you think about me going into business with Rah?"

"I think we should wait and see what the numbers are. But, either way, you should be careful when it comes to him in any way. I'd hate to have to kill him."

"You'd do that?" I asked, surprised.

"Don't seemed so shocked, Shay. You know I got real love for you. And I was the only one who saw how really ugly it was last time, so if this nigga ain't on the up and up its curtains for him."

I didn't say anything, I just wrapped, my arms around her. The definition of a true friend was so hard to find, that you really had to hold on tight to the ones you had.

"I love you for being you," I told her.

Our moment was interrupted by Raheem coming through the door pushing a cart with a few plates on it.

"I figured you both could use a little breakfast before we head back to the airport," he said.

"Where are my girls?" I asked, getting up so we could get dressed.

"I set them up at the hotel across the street so they wouldn't have far to travel. I figured we could switch them out every five to seven days, what do you think?"

"I think we need to see the money first," I replied.

"Of course," he said, pulling the lid off of one of the plates to reveal stacks of money.

Melissa did a quick count and checked bills at random until she was certain everything was straight.

"Fifty-thousand-dollars," she said, looking impressed.

"Fifty-thousand in one night?" I asked.

"Not even a full night," Rah said, smiling.

With those types of numbers, the decision wasn't hard—right or wrong, we were in business.

Aryanna

CHAPTER THIRTEEN

We decided to lay over for a little while and have a quick power brunch so I could meet his partners. After the night we'd had I didn't know if I was up to it, but Rah made the transaction smooth by having us go no further than the hotel restaurant.

Once we ironed out the particulars of where to wire the money, we handled the schedule of my girls rotating between two clubs here in Montreal, and one in Quebec, before they would head home. All in all, it was a power move that had taken place at the right time, and I'd gained enough to make up for the loss of my own club, and then some.

"I gotta say I'm pleasantly surprised," I told Rah, once we were on our way to the airport. It was just me, him and Melissa, because my girls didn't wanna waste any time getting back to the money.

"I bet you are," he replied, laughing.

"She ain't the only one," Melissa commented under her breath.

"People change. That's why I asked you to judge me based on my actions in the moment," he said, taking my hand.

There was a time not too long ago when I would've pulled away from him, or tried to beat his mufuckin' ass. The urge was still there to some degree, but now there was a competing force within that was telling me it was okay. *Was this just time healing old wounds? Was I dickmytized? Or was it just something about this nigga I couldn't shake no matter how hard I fought?* I couldn't quite put my finger on any one answer, but I knew caution was my best friend at this point.

When we finally made it back to the plane, I immediately headed for the couch for a much needed nap. But, it seemed as though just as soon as I'd shut my eyes, Melissa was poking me.

"What bitch?" I asked irritated.

"Why do I have like a million missed calls from Cliff?"

"Cliff? Why would he be calling you?" I wondered, already reaching for the phones in my purse. For the first time since we'd arrived, I realized how long it had been since I even thought about my phones, and that wasn't like me at all. If she had a million missed calls then mine probably totaled five-million between both phones! For him to be calling like that meant something wasn't right, so I quickly dialed his number.

"What's up, Cliff?"

"Shayna, were the fuck have you been? I've called around the world looking for your black ass!" he yelled.

"Calm down, negro, I had to take a last minute trip out of town. What's wrong?"

"What's wrong? Well, for starters, your truck was stolen and used in a crime."

"My truck? Who the fuck stole my truck?"

"We don't know yet because everyone has been operating under the assumption that you were driving it, and now you might be missing."

"Tell me what happened, and when it happened," I said, trying to organize my thoughts.

"Sometime last night, your truck was found in Dupoint Circle with something in it."

"Something in it? Something like what?" I asked. I could feel the hesitation coming heavy over the phone, but I wanted answers.

"Something like what?" I repeated.

"A-a-um- a head," he replied, slowly.

"A head of what?" I asked confused.

"Not a head of what. A head, as in the head of a human being."

The revelation left my tongue stuck to the roof of my mouth for a minute. Somebody's whole helmet, without the attached body, was found in my truck? That made absolutely no sense at all.

"What's going on, Shay?" Melissa asked. All I could do was shake my head at her as I continued to process what I'd just been told.

"Shay, are you there?" Cliff asked.

"Y-yeah, I'm just trying to make sense of what you're saying."

"There's more," he said

"Like what, the body?"

"No, we still don't know where the body is. Despite the gunshots to the face we were able to identify her with dental records."

"Her? It was a woman?" I asked, fear rolling heavy through my stomach as I pictured another one of my girl's losing her life.

"Don't worry it's not one of ours," he replied, obviously reading my mind.

"Okay, so what else is there Cliff, just spit it out."

"Her name was Camilla Austin," he said.

"Am I supposed to know who that is?"

"She was my first cousin," he replied, sadly.

"Oh. Damn. I'm sorry, Cliff. I didn't mean to sound insensitive about her or her death."

"Death?" Melissa echoed, giving me a what-the-fuck-look.

I put my finger to my lips in hopes that she would shut the fuck up so I could get the full story, but instead she headed for the front of the plane calling out for Rah. We were already taxing, but if I knew why she was gonna demand they put this mufucka in the air now.

"It's alright, I know you didn't know. You only met her once, and I think that was at our wedding a lifetime ago."

"Do you know why she was in my truck, or how she got there?" I asked.

"There are a lot of half-assed ideas floating around amongst homicide, but I personally think someone is sending a message."

"A message?" I asked, feeling a little more than uneasy. Because if someone was sending me a message that came in the form of a human head, the message could only mean one thing.

"Camilla had a son, who at one point in time, was best friends with our son," he explained.

"Okay, and?"

"And her son was the one Zo sent to fuck Makayla. He was the one who infected her with aids."

I allowed this revelation to roll around in my brain while I tried to make sense of it all. It was definitely a fucked up situation, but there wasn't any stretch of the imagination where I could see this message being mine or Cliff's. Nah, this was for Zo, which probably meant someone in Makayla's family heard he was back in town.

"Cliff, I think this was done to get Lorenzo's attention and run him out of town."

"Could be. I was panicked when I couldn't reach you though."

"I get it, but I was just out making business moves. I'll be home soon."

"Where are you now? It sounds like I hear an airplane."

"I'll explain everything later. Did the security cameras in the building see who stole my truck?"

"No, they were conveniently down for maintenance, but we're looking into it."

"Okay. I'll call you when I get home," I assured him.

"You better," he replied and hung up.

As soon as I got off the phone, Melissa was on my ass firing questions a mile a minute. I thought I was gonna have to slap her so she could take a breath. Once Rah joined us I ran the whole thing down to them, giving the little details I had.

"That's crazy," Rah said, echoing Melissa's words.

"Yeah, it is, but its DC. What's really crazy is that no matter where I'm at, I still can't escape Lorenzo's bullshit!"

"You know what you need? You need a vacation," Rah said, smiling.

"I been trying to tell her stubborn ass that, but she doesn't wanna listen to me or nobody else," Melissa said.

"That's because vacations don't pay the bills," I replied, seriously.

"Bitch, stop acting like you hurting for money. I'm your personal assistant so I know your net worth, probably more accurately then the IRS does."

"I mean, I'm doing a'ight, but I want that Oprah money."

"Shay, you can't hide that Oprah money, which means you need to learn to spend that shit sometimes," Rah said.

"I spend my money when I need to, thank you very much. Matter fact, Melissa, get on the phone and get me that new 2017 Jaguar XE to replace my Range Rover. I want it in Royal Blue," I ordered.

"Whatever you say, boss," she replied.

"What if you could take a vacation and make a little money too," Rah asked.

"How's that?"

"Well, if we went to Amsterdam for a while then we could relax with some of the best weed and women, plus bring some of your girls along for the ride."

"And let me guess, you know some people in Amsterdam?" I asked, smiling.

"A couple."

"Hmmm. Interesting proposition, but I'll have to think about it, okay?"

"Whatever you say, boss," he replied.

"Smartass. Now if you both will excuse me I gotta get some sleep before I start looking like a zombie."

Laying back down on the couch I gave serious thought to just getting away for a while. The knowledge that I could still make a dollar or two, made the idea all the more appealing, and in truth, the craziness that was DC was getting to me. I hadn't really travelled for myself since my trip to Jamaica, and that had been damn near two years ago.

By the time sleep found me I'd almost convinced myself that a trip was mandatory. My rest was dreamless and heavy, but sooner than I'd liked, Raheem was waking me up, telling me to get off the plane.

Melissa had the good sense to have Twan meet us on the Tarmac and we were on our way within minutes.

"Rah, Twan can drop you back at your car, but Melissa and I need to go to the office and get things straight with the girls."

"What you need to do is go home and take a soothing bath before you jump into all that. I'm sure it can wait until tomorrow," he replied.

"He's right, Shay," Melissa said.

I wanted to argue, but if the two of them were actually agreeing on something then I didn't have a leg to stand on.

"When do I get my car?" I asked.

"Tomorrow it'll be delivered."

"We getting a new toy?" Twan asked.

"Yeah, because somebody stole the Range Rover. I might be moving too if my building doesn't do something about their security."

"I heard that," Melissa said.

Twan took us all to my house where Melissa picked up her car and headed home. I thought Raheem would follow her lead, but I should've known that would be too much like right. I was too tired to fight his overprotective nature, plus a little pampering was good for me.

As soon as we walked through the door it was the Raheem show.I was instructed to sit on the couch while he made me a drink, put on some music, and ran me a bubble bath.

Before I knew it, I was relaxing in the hot water and smoking a blunt, while he bathed me with a gentleness I vividly remembered. Between the candle light and Prince blowing from my speakers, the nigga knew how to set a mood for seduction. I didn't even object, didn't say a word, as his hands caressed me thoroughly. I was so relaxed, I was tempted to go to sleep right there in the tub, but he made me get out before that happened.

Once he had me in my bedroom he dried me off, before rubbing oil onto my soft skin, from head to toe. There were no words for the therapy coming from his fingers, but he damn sure had me moaning from somewhere deep in my throat. I was anticipating him making a move that would turn intimacy into erotic fulfillment, but he didn't do it.

I was damn near disappointed until he undressed, climbed into bed with me and held me. Now I was scared to talk, deathly afraid of what might come out of my mouth while we were in this extremely vulnerable position. He knew me. He knew my secrets and my fears, just like he knew how to get to my heart. But, he didn't push. I felt the steady rhythm of his heart beating through me, and it was my last coherent thought as sleep claimed my conscious.

I fell hard and fast, dreaming of far off beaches and beautiful blue water. Even though I was sleeping deeply, I was wide awake the moment he pushed inside of me.

"Rah," I whispered, knowing we were both remembering moments like this.

"I know, baby," he rasped against my neck, letting his dick throb inside of me for a full minute before he pulled it out.

We used to go for hours just like this— slow strokes that pushed me to the point of tears. This wasn't about sex; he was determined to make love to me.

The rest of the night passed in a haze of heavy emotions and the sweetest release I'd experienced in years.

By the time the sun had risen, I knew real fear. In a twenty-four-hour window everything I thought I'd known and believed was now being questioned. The grown woman I'd become was locked in a death match with the little girl who believed in soulmates. Even trying to focus on the pain he'd caused wasn't having the usual affects. Only one thing in the world could be stronger and more deadly than denial, and that one thing was hope.

CHAPTER FOURTEEN

MEET ME IN THE MIRROR

What is it in me? Is it the man or animal that won't leave, that won't lie still, that's ready to kill those who bleed with the tenderness of a female, simply because the breed of me ain't what it used to be?

The analytical side of my mind tries to suppress this need to feed the savagery in me, hoping that with time I'll find a way to exist with self, because it's obvious there's two of me.

And while balance may be necessary, I feel this imbalance inside me. More man, or beast? I cannot say with certainty because after so many years of being lost, I don't know which of the two is more maddening! A man upright, independent and fearless by definition, but that just might be the right combination of wisdom to create havoc in a society where drones are preferred to those enlightened and on a mission.

My mission is missing though, lost in my mind because I can't see what need there is for me if I can't be accepted willingly for who I am.

Who I am? Man, beast, the question runs through my brain bringing me back to the same point in which I came with this pen to this paper. I know me and I know who I wanted to be, but it's days when these eyes see the ending of movies where the beginning is playing, erasing the mystery of how my story ends. It's those days that make me feel like I can't win, but I don't know too many men who won't fight simply because the odds are daunting.

Would it not haunt me more to wonder about the unexplored options of life, to wonder 'what if', or 'what could've been' because fighting seemed too hard? It's meant to be hard because I'm meant to be great, and given the obstacles I face it's no surprise that it's gonna take human, as well as animalistic traits to survive the harsh real-estate of the jungle I'm in.

I win just by fighting, not only outwardly, but the Demons in me that stroke the fires feeding the needs of brutality that are better left asleep. Not impossible, yet, far from easy. But, the sacrifices made are not in vain if man and beast co-exist in the same body, on the same plane of metal and spiritual enlightenment, and mold the boy or girl who seeks to claim that in which they truly don't understand. This life...this game.

Dear M,

I never thought you were ungrateful when it came to how you responded to my gift. I know it was a complete shock to you, especially considering that it never came up in conversation, but you deserve to be happy. I'm glad you're okay with it now though, and you'll be pleased to know that I'm nowhere near done. Anything worth doing is worth doing right.

As for the distance between us, I wish we lived closer too. The good news is that everything will be just like it should be in another two weeks. I feel like a little kid waiting on Christmas with the way I'm counting down! Lol! Can you blame me?

To say that I've missed you is the understatement of a lifetime, and I know you feel the same way. There's so much I wanna, so once you're here, I have the feeling that a vacation for just the two of us will be necessary. Don't worry, I've already started planning it and I can promise you the time of your life.

Until then, I want you to just relax, with no worries, because I'm gonna take care of everything. I promise.

Whoever said 'good things come to those who wait' knew what they were talking about, because living in the moment is truly magical. I'm glad we're sharing it together. I love you, and I'll be in touch soon.

Love always,

J.R.

Aryanna

CHAPTER FIFTEEN

The sounds of someone banging on my front door woke me from a peaceful sleep, and instantly pissed me off. Raheem was sound asleep behind me, which meant that whoever my unexpected visitor was, better be prepared to get cussed the fuck out.

Hopping out of bed I threw on Rah's shirt, buttoning it as I made my way to the door and looked out the peephole.

"What the fuck, Cliff!" I said, snatching the door open.

"You were supposed to call me when you got home."

"Okay, I forgot, but that don't give you the right to be up here beating my shit down early in the morning.

"Early in the morning? Shayna, it's two in the dame afternoon," he replied, looking at me concerned.

I turned back to the living room in search of a clock, knowing he had to be wrong because there was no way I'd slept the day away like that. My phones were on the coffee table and both read 2:07 p.m., along with a lot of missed calls from my girls, Melissa, Cliff and my mom.

"Wow," was all I could say.

"See? Now don't you owe me an apology?" he asked. The look I gave him said 'nigga please' in any language, and he was smart enough not to press the issue.

"Anyway, I just wanted to make sure you were okay," he said, closing the door and joining me in the living room.

"I'm fine, but now ain't a good time," I replied, knowing Rah could wake up any minute.

"It's never a good time, Shayna."

"I've got company, Cliff."

"And? I'm not here for no pussy, we need to talk."

"Okay fine, talk."

"Well, there's no word on Camilla, and her body hasn't been found. There's still no word on Lorenzo, which is looking like a better thing for all of us with each passing day. The explosion at the club came from some type of device that was set off in the kitchen. No one knows how long it's there, but it was triggered remotely."

"Anything else?" I asked.

"No, that's it for now. What have you been working on?"

"Just making sure the girls have somewhere to dance until the club is rebuilt."

"Oh, yeah? Where are they dancing?"

"I know some people with a few clubs up north," I replied vaguely, hoping he'd let go at that.

"Up north? Why would you-."

"Babe, I need my shirt," Rah said, coming into the living room. As soon as Cliff saw him, the tension was on one-thousand.

"This is your company? Why would you fuck with this nigga again, Shay? You know he ain't shit!"

"Cliff," I said in a warning tone.

"Nah, it's okay, Shayna, let him speak," Raheem said, taking a seat on the couch.

"I don't got shit to say to you, nigga, except if you hurt her this time, you gonna have to see me."

"You ain't gotta worry about me hurting her, but I can take a strong look at you right now if you like," Rah said, standing up.

"Are you mufuckas serious right now? Raheem sit your ass down, and Cliff I'll talk to you later," I said, going to the front door, and opening it for him.

"Yeah, a'ight," was his reply as he left.

No sooner had the door shut, I spun on Rah, ready to lay into his ass.

"What the fuck was that? You wanna get into a dick swinging contest with my partner?" To my surprise he unbuttoned his slacks and let them drop to his ankles, revealing he didn't have on any underwear.

"There's no contest when it come to this dick, and you know it," he said, smiling.

I made the mistake of looking at his beautiful package which allowed all my thoughts to fly south for the summer. He was definitely in a class all by himself! Still, I couldn't let that affect my money.

"Look man, I need Cliff and if you wanna stay in business with me then you need him too. In other words, don't start no shit, or you're gonna find yourself by yourself, feel me?"

He crossed the room and made his way over to me. Then, he turned me around until he had my back pulled up against his chest.

"I apologize, sweetheart," he murmured in my ear, grabbing a fistful of my hair.

"I'm serious, Raheem," I said, feeling my knees tremble a little.

"I know you are," he said, bending me over, "and I feel you," he grunted, as he plowed into me hard enough to raise me up on my tippy toes. As soon as he pulled back for his next blow, my phone started to ring and it took everything in me to climb off the dick.

"H-hello?" I panted.

"'Bout time you answered the damn phone!"

"I'm sorry, Mom. I over slept by a lot. Are you okay?"

"I'm fine, just wondering what the hell has been going on with you."

"It's been hectic, but I've just been handing business as usual."

"Uh-huh. All of a sudden you don't got time for me?"

"Come on, Mom. You know it ain't like that."

"Good, so then I can expect you at my house for a late lunch then, right?"

"Yes, Ma'am," I replied, smiling at how easy she maneuvered me into that.

"Be here in an hour. Oh, and bring Raheem with you too."

"Rah? I don't know-."

"Shayna, you never were a good liar so don't start trying now, baby. I'll see you in an hour," she said, hanging up.

"What did she say?" Rah asked.

"She said we have an hour to get to her house for a late lunch. Did you tell her anything about us?"

"Seriously? You know damn well I wouldn't do that and give her any type of false hope."

"So how the hell does she know?" I wondered aloud.

"Because she's Ida Mae," he replied, taking my hand, leading me into the bathroom.

Ida Mae was definitely a force to be reckoned with. I just didn't wanna feel any pressure about whatever was happening between me and Rah. Pressure busted pipes.

We took a shower that lasted longer than necessary, for obvious reasons, but still managed to make it to my Mom's with five minutes to spare.

Mom had a lay out of crabs and shrimp, which was a meal we all used to share together, once upon a time. The stroll down memory lane was powerful and surprisingly painless.

We all spent the next couple of hours eating and laughing, each telling stories funnier than the last, and more embarrassing.

I was honestly sad to have it come to an end, but my mother made sure to secure inner plans for later in the week.

I thought Rah and I would leave together, but to my surprise, he gave me a thorough kiss and put me into my car. He said he knew I had work to do, especially with regards to the net batch of girls we had going to Canada. Plus, he wanted to give me the chance to miss him a little.

I thought that was the funniest shit in the world until I found myself lying in bed that night rubbing my clit, wondering what he was doing. Any woman 'bout the dick will tell you that once you're getting it right, your body starts calling for it like an old R. Kelly song.

Within a matter of hours, I was feeling the effects of the withdrawals, but I wasn't about to tell that nigga the truth. I even went so far as to scan through my phone for some of the dick I had on tap, but none of it could measure up, so what was the point?

In the end, it was a cold shower, followed by a fat blunt, and a downloaded book by Reds Johnson that got me through the night.

The next two days passed in a somewhat similar fashion, which had a bitch light-way cranky, but I focused my time and energy on work. My girls were more than happy to make the trip to Canada, especially when they reached out to the ones already up there and heard the numbers.

My account wasn't looking too shabby either, which, of course, had me thinking about a long term investment in the Canadian real-estate market. Something to discuss with Raheem, whenever I saw his ghostly ass again.

Day three of me not seeing him had me start my day off wondering if menopause had reversed itself and I was on my period. I was all types of agitated until Melissa burst into my office with a huge bouquet of red roses.

"What's this?" I asked, accepting them.

"I don't know. They were delivered for you with this envelope." Opening the envelope, I found a poem.

PLEASE

I could see us being history in the making if we let history remake we, bringing the past love believed to be lost, into a future bright with limitless possibilities of happiness unseen. Can you see it, feel it? With the elevated beat of my heart I envisioned, clearly, tomorrow and the day after, the next chapters in the book of our forever. It's evident we were meant to be on entity divided by nothing and no one, in this world, or beyond.

Before you respond hastily, allow me to draw my vision, hopefully allowing your heart its needed moment of clarity. To hell and back we've been, sometimes bending rules in terms of forbidden love viewed by eyes unworthy of seeing the beauty we create. Mistakes were made, cards misplayed, but we only lose if we quit the game of love and life completely, and baby, I can't see why we would do that.

Our ability is to bounce back from whatever, be it relationships or doing time. It's plain to see that time and again we're drawn together, watching life's difficulties as one unit, which clearly communicates the need for what we give each other.

I say need, not, want, because at this point frontin' does no good for the overall mission in which winning and defying the odds is our ambition. We can have an incredible life, that vision you saw as a little girl about being a wife cherished by her husband is not something you have to miss out on.

All I need is that in which I'm giving— my heart and love without condition or reservation, because this life I'm living without you is wasted. It can't be better to have saved and lost, the cost of losing you was too much to ask and that's why I've never gotten pass the past, or over you.

To start anew using the path taken as our map or foundation is what I'm asking you now because somehow, someway, your love isn't something shakable or worthy of faking that I can do without. Don't let the fact that I say 'I' confuse you as to whether I'm thinking about 'We', because I'm trying to get you to see that me alone doesn't exist.

You're the air I breath, and it's only your complete love that's ever made me the man I need to be.

So baby, I'm asking, suggesting, shit, you can even say I'm begging, for history's kiss to grace my lips in the form of you returning to be my everything.

Royalty we were, but a king is nothing without his queen...

I read it again, absolutely mesmerized by the honesty and raw emotion he'd put on display. In all the years I'd known him he'd never done this. Don't get me wrong, there had been grand gestures and romance before, but never had he been this vulnerable with me.

"What it say?" Melissa asked.

For a moment, I'd forgotten she was here. This man's words had transported me to a world of my own and I'd halfway expected him to be standing in front of me instead of her.

"It's nothing," I replied softly.

"Uh-huh, bitch, I can see all thirty-two of your teeth right now. Is it from Raheem?"

"Yes, it's all from Rah, and that's all the info your ass is getting."

"Ugh! You wanna be all secretive and shit," she said with an attitude, as she left my office.

I wasn't about to let her fuck up my mood though because right now I was feeling some type of way about Mr. Raheem. He seemed to be full of surprises, and not just in a business sense either. I knew what he was trying to do though, with his slick ass.

After reading the poem one more time, I sat it on my desk and inhaled the sweet scent of my flowers. I put them in a vase and sat them in the window, and then I tried to refocus my thoughts on work.

I could tell I wasn't doing a good job because an hour later I caught myself daydreaming about fucking the shit out of this nigga. He must've felt me thinking about him because my phone vibrated with a text from him asking how my day was going. I told him it was interesting, hoping to down play the feeling of butterflies he was giving me. He laughed at my interesting comment and asked what time I got off.

I'd originally planned to work late, but then shit was about to go out the window if he said anything like he was trying to do something. Not to seem too thirsty, I kept my response to 'I don't know' and asked him why. He didn't hit me right back, and before I could call him, my phone was ringing with security asking me to come downstairs because there was a problem involving my car. That was the last fucking thing I wanted to hear after spending one-hundred-thousand dollars to get my new Jag the way I wanted it.

Grabbing my purse, I headed for the elevator, telling Melissa what the problem was, on my way. As soon as I hit the lobby, I knew something was up because there stood Raheem with another bouquet of roses.

"What's this?" I asked, trying in vain to hide my smile.

"Just a little something to put that smile back on your face. I knew you'd be pissed thinking something was wrong with your car."

"Ah, so that was all your doing?"

"It was, but it was so worth it. I had to see you now," he said, kissing my lips tenderly. I could feel my heart beating in my stomach, but I willed myself to remain calm.

"Well, now that you see me, what's next?" I asked.

"I need you to do something that doesn't come natural to you. I need you to relax and let me take control." He knew exactly what he was asking, but he was smart enough not to use words that would get him immediately rejected.

He wanted me to trust him. I didn't voice any of this, but instead, I nodded my head to demonstrate my willingness.

Arm in arm, we walked outside where my car waited. Apparently, Twan knew more than me because he didn't ask for directions once we were in the backseat, he just sped off into traffic. The music in the car was something like Luther Vandross' greatest hit, and Rah sang softly to me the whole ride. A man that can sing will have a woman out of her panties in no time, and let me tell you I thought I was gonna ruin my leather seats because this man had me wet!

In what seemed like minutes, we were in Baltimore at the Port. Once we stepped out of the car, he led the way along the dock until we stopped next to a yacht that had to be at least two-hundred feet long. The name on it was The Payback.

"Uh, Rah, what are we doing?" I asked.

"We're reconnecting," he replied.

"Oh, yeah, and how are we doing that?"

"Close your eyes and I'll show you."

I did as he asked, wondering what else he had up his sleeve.

"Okay, open them," he said.

I did like I was told, but what I saw didn't make sense. In his hand he held a box, and in that box there was a ring.

Aryanna

CHAPTER SIXTEEN

"Raheem," I whispered, terrified to say more than that.

"Before you panic, I just want you to hear me out first. I knew that no matter what, when we had this conversation it was gonna seem too soon, because all the pain I caused you is still fresh in your mind. So, what I'm proposing is that we take a trip, just the two of us, where we can really get reacquainted and make some new memories. All I'm asking for at this moment is your time," he concluded, taking my hand and slipping the ring on my finger.

It was stunning, and it looked like I was wearing a piece of the sun. I'd lost count of how many times I'd played this scenario out in my mind since that first day our eyes had met in that courtroom. If I was gonna be honest with myself, I'd always known that it wasn't the act of cheating that had destroyed me; I could've gotten past that. No, what had hurt the most was the fact that he'd given another woman what was only meant for me.

He was supposed to be my husband forever, and knowing some other bitch had snuck in and robbed me was enough to turn my heart to stone. Yet, here we stood all these years later, and as unbelievable as it seemed, a second chance was only a word away. Could I answer him? I mean, technically, he hadn't popped the question, but there was no doubt in either of our minds what waited at the end of this boat ride.

At the moment, my heartbeat sounded like the boom of a tractor-trailer's air horn in my ears. For a fleeting minute I thought I was gonna throw up, but a bitch wouldn't show weakness like that. If I asked myself what I had to lose, my immediate answer would be my goddamn mind. But, if I didn't take this chance, I'd also lose him.

Beyoncé had dropped a song about situations like this called *Dangerously in Love,* and I was hearing it right now, as I took in the beautiful water dancing with the sun's illumination.

"Lord help me," I murmured.

"Is that a yes?" he asked.

"Uh, can you repeat the question?"

"The question is will you spend some time with me?" he replied, laughing.

"How much time, Rah?"

"Eventually, forever, but for now we'll start with a few weeks. Before you argue let me explain the full plan. We start off by making our way through the Caribbean Island, hopping and partying for a week or two. Then, we set sail for Amsterdam where, at least, twenty of your top workers will meet us. I've actually arranged for them to head over there within the next week, so not only will they be waiting on you, but so will a nice amount of money."

"How much we talking?" I asked intrigued.

"Same percentages as Canada. And before you say anything, I've already talked to your mom and let her know we'll be gone for three or four weeks."

"So you thought of everything, huh?"

"Allow me to show you," he said, taking my hand and leading me aboard the yacht.

It was truly magnificent, pearl white with what looked like twenty-four karat gold trim on everything. It sat two stories high and looked like it was wide enough for six lane traffic to run through it. The dining room table was set for two, and we enjoyed a leisurely lunch of steak, baked potato, and a Cesare Salad, with a bottle of red wine to compliment the meal.

The staff moved around us, whispering quietly, never allowing an empty glass, or an empty plate to linger. Throughout the meal, I caught myself looking at Raheem and smiling, enjoying his company as much as I did the weight of the diamond on my finger.

After we ate he led me below deck where there were five bedrooms, including a master suite. I admired the other rooms in passing because they were done tastefully in burgundy and gold.

But, when we got to the master suite I thought my eyes would pop out of my head. There was a king size bed, front and center, and it was covered in red, white, and yellow rose petals. They looked so beautiful reflecting off the mirror that was on the ceiling. Even more impressive than that, was the fact that every inch of the floor was covered in money, and I don't mean as a carpet design; there were literally one-hundred-dollar bills scattered all over the damn floor!

"Is that real?" I asked.

"Of course it is, why would you ask that?"

"I mean, why is it on the floor then? I don't understand."

"For a couple of reasons. One, is because money is beneath you and it will never hold more value to me than you do. Secondly, because I can offer you any material thing in the world, but what I really wanna give you is love."

I had no response to what he'd said. It was obvious to me that this man wasn't plying and he was pulling out all the stops. At that moment, I knew what he'd probably already seen as a forgone conclusion— I wasn't getting off this boat.

"When do we leave?" I asked.

"When you're ready."

"You've got my time, let's do it."

Meanwhile...

The sounds of the gate clanging shut behind me for the last time was music to my ears. I never thought I'd see the day, and in truth, for a while I hadn't wanted to. If I'd learned nothing else in this lifetime, it was that dying was the easy part because living was a mufucka.

As I passed through the last gate and looked towards the parking lot I saw my reason for living right where he'd said he'd be. I couldn't put into words how much I distrusted this man, but I knew this was one man who would always have my back.

As soon as I got near him, I leapt into his arms and held him close, feeling my tears fall like gun shells while reality set in a little more. This was happening, this was really fucking happening!

"I've missed you so much," I sobbed, unable to stop crying now that I'd finally opened the flood gates. I couldn't even remember the last time I'd let myself cry, but they were tears of joy, so it was okay.

"I missed you too, and I'm so glad you're finally home," he said, holding me close.

"Can we get out of here, now?" I asked.

"You ain't gotta say it twice, your chariot awaits," he replied, stepping back so I could see the car.

"Is that a Rolls?'

"Yep."

"Is it yours?"

"No, it's yours."

"Why would you spend all that money?" I asked in awe.

"Oh, I didn't pay a dime for it. Shayna wanted you to have it." Hearing this made me laugh, but I admired her taste in cars as I slid into the passenger seat. The ride was smooth too, and I was taking it all in.

Everything was so different, even the air tasted different from the recycled bullshit I'd been breathing. Riding through DC was like coming home to a place I'd never been because so much had changed. I was trying to take it all in at once without overwhelming myself, because the psychologist had told me that I could trigger a PTSD episode if I became too stressed. I knew I couldn't spend my life hiding in a corner, so it was best to get acclimated as quickly as possible.

"So, where are we going?" I asked.

"Where do you wanna go first?"

That was a good question. I'd thought about it a lot, and I'd never put a firm idea in my mind. Maybe because I didn't know if this day would really come, or maybe because I didn't wanna give myself any hope. Either way, the time had finally come, the day was here, and the world was now at my feet.

"I guess the first thing I need to do is go shopping."

"I love you, but are you really about to make me go shopping with you?" he asked, laughing.

"Yep! I'm not letting you out of my sight today, so you better suck it up and smile."

"Yes ma'am!"

"Good. Now, you're gonna have to navigate this shopping expedition because it's obvious I have no idea where to go."

"No problem, but if we're doing this then we're gonna do it right."

"What does that mean?" I asked warily.

"Just trust me, I got you."

I did trust him with my life, so it wasn't hard to sit back and enjoy the ride. He made one phone call to someone and told them to get ready because we were coming to take a shopping trip, but he still didn't say where we were going. I was cool just enjoying the sights and the sounds of the world around me. A lot had changed in terms of fashion too, because dudes were wearing jeans as tight as the women were wearing.

"Damn, with niggas jeans so tight where they hiding their guns at?" I asked. This made him laugh hysterically for a few minutes.

"I swear I be wondering the same shit, but those rappers got dudes thinking it's cool."

"I know you better not be rockin' no skin tights," I said laughing.

"Now you know I ain't for none of that."

We stopped at McDonalds to get something to eat, and I actually ordered one of everything, even though I knew I couldn't eat it all. A lot may have changed, but I was still five-foot-one-inches tall and one-hundred-thirty pounds. I didn't consider myself as cute or as beautiful as I once was, but I knew I could still turn heads if I wanted to; I didn't want to though. I'd gotten used to being invisible, and it transformed what others saw as a slight into my identity.

Only certain people could understand the power of going unseen, and for me, it was about survival. I doubted my outlook would ever change when it came to this fact. As soon as our food came through the window, I was about my business trying to make up for lost time. It may not have been lady like to gobble my food the way I was, but I guarantee any mufucka who judged me hadn't spent time behind the wall. I was so caught up in my food that it took me a while to notice when we'd pulled up at the airport.

"What are we doing here?" I asked.

"We're gonna take a quick trip to New York and do some shopping," he replied, casually.

"New York? I can't just leave town like that, you know that."

"Will you relax? I promise we'll be back in a few hours."

I didn't argue, but I was leery the whole way through the terminal and out onto the private jet. I kept expecting someone to leap out and snatch me, sending me back to hell without a second thought. That didn't happen though.

Instead, I spent four straight hours having the time of my fucking life, finally getting rid of some of the shadows that had haunted me. We shopped, we laughed, we blew money like it was going out of style, and it felt amazing!

By the time we got back to the city I was positive my life was worth living, and I was damn sure gonna live everyday like it was my last.

"So where is he?" I asked, as we cruised the streets of southeast.

"Well, I figured it should end where it began. The problem with that was that the National's Baseball Stadium is where your spot use to be, so I had to settle for southwest."

"Is it secluded?"

"Yeah, I had it sound proofed all the way through."

"Take me there," I ordered. I'd done a lot of reading, especially the good book, and I knew that forgiveness was more for me than for the other person, the thing with me though was, I didn't want forgiveness. Not for me, not for anyone involved. I wanted justice.

When we pulled up in front of the house it finally hit me that the beginning of my new life would truly start once I walked through that door. I'd actually chosen one of my new outfits for the occasion. I stepped out of the car in a Gucci jean body suit with low cut Gucci boots. For the first time in longer than I could remember, I felt like a woman in my own skin. Who knows, maybe I would grow my hair back out.

"You ready?" he asked.

"Lead the way," I replied, following him up the steps and into the house.

The house was nice and really spacious, especially considering the fact that there was no furniture anywhere. The living room and dining room were completely dark, and I could see where the windows had been boarded up from the inside.

The only light on was the one in the hallway. There were four bedroom doors spaced out about four-feet apart, with two on each side of the hallway.

We came to the first door on our left and he unlocked it. I was ready to walk in, but a sickening smell rushed out at me, making me gag and gasp at the same time.

"What is that?" I asked.

"That's him."

"Damn, is he still alive?"

"Yeah, but he may have been fucked one or two hundred times in the last month."

"Mmph. That nigga is funky," I said, finally stepping into the room with my hand over my face. I heard him chuckling behind me.

In front of me there was a naked man handcuffed to a four posted bed, and it was evident that both him and his ass had seen better days. Any normal person might feel bad for him in this situation, but I wasn't normal and I owed that to him.

"You awake?" I called out sweetly.

"No more. Please, no more," he sobbed.

"I never thought I'd hear the day when all the bitch came out of you, Slim. Not you," I taunted.

"Who-who's that?"

"Hit the lights JR," I said, stepping to the side of the bed so our prisoner could see exactly who I was. For a long minute all he did was look through me, but then his eyes focused and I saw recognition. Recognition turned to disbelief, and disbelief turned to fear, until all his eyes showed was pure terror.

"It can't be," he said.

"Oh, it can be, but I bet you wish it wasn't. Did you miss me, Lorenzo?"

"M-Makayla, please. Please!"

Aryanna

CHAPTER SEVENTEEN

I was living a dream. My life had literally transformed into the shit movies were made of, filled with good food, beautiful scenery, and amazing sex. Our sex life had always been lit, but this mufucka was going above and beyond to keep me satisfied; I was getting the complete package.

He ate my pussy at least twice a day, I got intimate massages and foot rubs, and at night, he made love to me with such passion, that a few times I had to cry. Making love on a yacht in the rain, in the middle of the ocean, was an experience I'd never find the words to describe. All I knew was that Raheem wasn't leaving anything to chance when it came to convincing me to marry him.

It wasn't all about the sex though. We actually talked about a lot of different things, from work to what the future could possibly look like five to ten years from now. We discussed the Presidential Election between Donald Trump and Hilary Clinton, as well as what we could do to support the Black Lives Matter Movement.

Somewhere in between when we'd broken up and now, Raheem had polished the edges of his versatility, and the young boy was now definitely all man, by any definition. I loved it!

And even though I swore I wouldn't do it, I could feel myself coming to love him more and more with each passing day. By the end of the first week, I was sucking his dick so much that I was on a steady diet of cum as my source of protein. By the end of the second week, anything he asked of me came with a response of 'yes daddy'. I was open, but the truth was I didn't care. Nobody was around to judge me, so I let myself get comfortable in my own skin, finally admitting what I'd known for so very long— I was gone for this nigga.

Shit, the truth was that when I looked in the mirror I saw more lines on my face, but these were laughing lines. Was this happiness? I dared to breath the word!

Our next stop was the Bahamas before we made the turn for Europe to meet up with my girls, and I was actually thinking about switching up the game a little. I already knew he wore a size ten in rings, so it wouldn't be hard to get him a little something that said I was jumping in with both feet. I wanted to run the idea past my mom and Melissa, but I hadn't been able to catch up with them.

Lying here on the deck working on my tan was one of the rare free moments I got, but the fact that he was sleeping right next to me meant anything could pop off. Looking at him now, and observing just how handsome he was, I wondered if I could see myself waking up next to him every morning. In my opinion, the biggest obstacle of marriage was boredom, but I didn't foresee that problem in our relationship.

Rah could be maddening and make a bitch wanna shoot first and ask questions last, but he was far from boring. *So what's holding me back?* Even as I ask myself this I don't hear the usual warning bells or screams of terror. Maybe I was ready. Lord help me, but somewhere along the way I'd tripped and landed head-first in love with this sexy mufucka beside me.

This was definitely a dangerous position to be in because the hardening of my heart after his betrayal is what had made me a monster when it came to business. *Who would I be now?* Rainbows and butterflies didn't pimp hoes, especially not the strong niggas I had opposite my females on the payroll. I couldn't lose my edge. Then again, Rah was a part of the business now, and in the interest of growing the empire, he'd have to make sure I kept my edge— steel sharpened steel, it was that simple.

So all this heavy thinking brought me around to the conclusion my subconscious had reached a while ago. I was going to marry this nigga. The realization didn't come with the blinding illumination of lightening or the force of thunder, it just kinda slid into place. That told me there was already room for that type of craziness in my mind. I could see the island of the Bahamas in the distance, and I wondered if an impromptu wedding right here would be the thing to do. I mean, my mom and close friends might feel some type of way, but there was also less of a chance of objections and bullshit.

The more the idea rolled around in my head, the more I liked it. Now it was just time to inform the groom-to-be. Getting up from my lounge chair, I bent over his naked body and took his dick into my mouth. It only took a few seconds before he was rock hard and moaning in his sleep. My next move was to get on his lounge chair with him and then on top of him; the moment I took him deep inside me he was wide awake looking up at me.

"Mmm, hello to you too, sweetheart," he murmured, grabbing my hips.

"Baby, I was-was thinking," I said, trying to keep my concentration as he started lifting up into me.

"About?"

For a second I was lost, but I took the control back with a swivel of my hips. "About us getting married."

"W-What are y-you saying, babe?" he stammered.

"I'm saying yes," I replied, riding him faster.

"O-Okay." I could tell by the look in his eyes that he was getting ready to unleash, so I came to a screeching halt.

"Why you stop, Shay?"

"Because I wanna marry you."

"Baby, I said okay. I promise you I won't change my mind," he replied, trying to get me to move again.

"I wanna get married today," I told him.

"What?"

"You heard me, Rah."

"Yeah, I heard you, but are you sure?"

"As sure as I am of this," I told him, rising slowly, until only the tip of him was pulsating inside me, before slamming myself back down on him.

I did that twice more before his eyes threatened to roll back like Walmart prices, and he agreed without hesitation. Before I knew it, he had me up and bent over the railing, pounding me as the beauty of the Bahamas came into clear view.

We sailed into Port with me getting my back blown out, and nothing had ever turned me on that much in my life. I didn't want it to end, but I saw people with their phones out, and I knew we could be a viral sensation within minutes. Not a good look for my legit business.

We hurried down the stairs, but I knew everyone within a mile had heard us climax together.

"Okay, you make the legal arrangements and I have some quick shopping to do," I told him, pulling out a flowery sundress with white pen toed sandals.

I didn't wanna waste time with a bank so I grabbed a couple stacks of the money we had laying around, and set off to pull the perfect wedding together in a day.

The hardest part would forever be the dress, but I got off lucky because at my first stop I found a beautiful flowing, floor length, white, strapless dress by Vera Wang. It was gonna be long on my short frame, but having a juicy ass was gonna help a little. With the dress out of the way, I hit the jewelry store to accessorize, snatching up some two karat diamond studs and a matching diamond heart pendant on a platinum chain. I even managed to find the perfect diamond encrusted wedding band for him, which only left me to find him something to wear.

I had to make my way through three different shops before I found the perfect all white linen Versace short ensemble that would perfectly compliment my dress. The receipts in my pocket said I ran through twenty-two thousand dollars, but what I was getting for my money was priceless. I was tempted to stop for a quick bite to eat, but if I knew my man, he'd already made some type of dinner reservations. He was thoughtful like that.

As soon as I got back to the docks I saw the man in question standing on the dock, waiting patiently for me.

"Hi, beautiful," he said, pulling me to him for a long kiss.

"Mmph. Hi yourself, what was that for?"

"I just missed you, that's all. How did shopping go?"

"Oh my God, bae, I got the most beautiful dress, but you can't see it until I put it on."

"Okay, go put it on for me," he replied, kissing my neck.

"No, not until our wedding day."

"Oh, well then I guess I'll have to wait until tomorrow then."

"You got the marriage license?' I asked, eagerly.

"Downstairs in the safe, and I found a priest to do the ceremony on the beach. The only decision left to make is what time you'd like to say, I do."

"Hmm… How about sunrise? I wanna be Mrs. Raheem Miles A.S.A.P.!"

"I'm definitely cool with that, especially since I made a decision you might not agree with."

"Oh yeah, and what's that?" I asked, pulling back so I could look into his eyes. Thankfully, I didn't see deceit, but instead a hint of mischief.

"Well, I reserved a suite at the best hotel in town."

"Ooh, is it the honeymoon suite?"

"It is, but it'll be used before then. By you."

"Come again?" I said, slightly confused.

"I wanna take the somewhat old fashioned approach to this, so we're gonna spend tonight apart."

As grown as I was, I couldn't help the pout I knew was on my face. I could feel my bottom lip sticking out farther than Bubba's in Forest Gump! A night apart may not seem like a lot, but a bitch was spoiled. Between the hours of 12 a.m. to 10 a.m. I got more loving than most chicks did in a month, and it was Campbell Soup, mmm-mmm good! Now he was asking me to go without? How did he expect me to sleep?

"But, baby, you know I'll be restless and stressed, and I don't wanna bring those kinda feelings into our wedding day," I reasoned.

"I understand, but think about how great it's gonna be to-morrow night. Plus, I've got something for you that'll get you through tonight," he replied, leading me below deck to our room.

As soon as we walked through the door I smelled the bud, and it was a force to be reckoned with.

"What the fuck is that?" I asked.

"That is my pre-wedding gift to you," he replied, passing me a pound of weed wrapped in plastic.

I didn't waste any time sitting my bags down, taking the weed from him, and finding a blunt to twist on up. The hairs on the weed were a mixture of purple and red, and it was sticky to the touch. All of these things pointed to this being some serious bud, which definitely would help with my stress for tonight.

"Not so fast, sweetheart, we've got dinner reservations for two," he said, removing the weed from my lap.

"Aww, can't I blow one?"

"Not of this shit, you can smoke some of what you been smoking. This shit right here be putting these niggas dick in the dirt around here, and I want you completely coherent for the next few hours."

I wanted to pout again, but then I thought about all we could accomplish with the time we had left. I didn't argue when he led me to the shower and we got clean, then dirty, then clean all over again.

We went to a restaurant called Soul's and enjoyed good food, good champagne, and each other's company. Truthfully, it already felt like the honeymoon, but I knew whatever Rah had planned would pale in comparison to what we had now. Still, he'd made sure to rent out the entire back half of the restaurant, which gave us plenty of privacy and room for frisky behavior.

"You never get enough do you?" he asked, when I grabbed his dick under the table.

"You know the answer to that question," I purred in his ear,

For now, we were just teasing each other. He fed me lobster, and I licked the butter from his fingers. He'd talked me into wearing my vibrating underwear and when I least expected it, I got the shock of a lifetime. By the time he escorted me to the hotel room, I was beyond ready for him to dance all up inside of me.

"You coming?" I asked, when he just stood at the open hotel room door.

"Not tonight, baby."

"Uh-uh, Rah, you can't send me to bed like this," I protested, grabbing his hand.

"We made a deal, bae. I already had everything you need delivered to the room, and I'll see you before you know it."

Raheeeemmm," I whined, putting on my sexiest pout.

"I'm sorry, baby. I love you," he replied, lifting my hand to his lips and kissing it.

For a moment I thought I saw real tears in his eyes, but before I could say anything he was already heading down the hallway. I watched him until he was no more than my imagination, and then I closed the door, hoping tomorrow would hurry up and get here.

In my room, I found a huge queen size bed, a fifty-inch plasma on the wall, a fruit basket on the nightstand, and a bottle of champagne chilling on the table that led to the balcony. My shopping bags were on the bed, as well as my weed.

I poured me a glass of champagne and rolled a blunt, before stepping onto the balcony to enjoy the view. It was absolutely stunning, watching the sky go from orange to purple as the sun set, and to see that reflecting off of the beautiful water.

The Bahamas was coming alive with the nightlife, and the music tempted me to go out and party a little. I'd save that as a last resort if I couldn't relax like I wanted to. For now, I was content to fire this good green, kick back in one of the two wicker chairs, and enjoy my drink. Before I was halfway through the blunt I could feel its potent affect smack me in the face, which should've been my cue to put it out, but I kept blowing.

By the time I was finished, I was in desperate need of a refill on my drink because a bitch had serious cotton mouth. When I stood up, the world tilted and my beautiful view took on a different angle as I saw the sky from my back.

Luckily for me, I'd fallen back into my hotel room. Rah had warned me that this shit was powerful, but I ain't never smoked nothing that put me on my ass like this. The thing was, the high wasn't letting up; it was intensifying with each passing moment. Two failed attempts at standing told me really quick that travel was only gonna be accomplished on all fours, and the only direction I needed to go in was the bedroom.

Time didn't make sense so I don't know how long it took me, but eventually, I was able to pull myself up onto the bed. My last coherent thought was of how beautiful my wedding dress was, and then everything got real dark.

When I woke up, I felt pain behind my eyes and the drums in my ears were so loud I had to convince myself to think in a whisper. That wasn't a hangover. I didn't know what it was, but one blunt and glass of bubbly shouldn't have made me feel like death.

One of the two had to have been laced, but I couldn't see Raheem doing that to me. I tried to open my eyes, but I felt like I was looking directly into the sun through a telescope. All I could do was lay in the fetal position, hoping normalcy would find me so I wouldn't have to go looking for it.

After what seemed like the longest fifteen minutes of my life, I tried again to open my eyes, and I was able to keep them open long enough to locate the bathroom. Praying for strength, I stumbled and fumbled my way to the bathroom where I grabbed onto the toilet and held it like I loved it, throwing up so hard I thought I had whiplash.

I wouldn't stop, I mean, it was coming through my nose and mouth at the same time, making breathing almost impossible. This lasted for an agonizing five minutes, and then I was finally able to release the toilet long enough to get better acquainted with the marble floor. The coolness of it stopped my momentary prayers for death.

I could slowly feel my body temperature returning to normal and then came the beginnings of coherent thought. I didn't know what had fucked me up, but unless I was crazy, the bright sun in the sky meant I was late for my own wedding. And where the hell was Raheem? After another ten minutes on the floor, I was able to put my equilibrium to the test and stand up, making my way back into the bedroom.

The first thing I did was check my phone. The time said it was 11 a.m., but even more surprising than that, was the fact that I had no missed calls from Rah. I tried calling him, but it didn't even ring before it went to voicemail which meant his phone wasn't on.

As quickly as my still delicate condition would allow, I put the weed in one of my shopping bags, tucked the bags under the bed, grabbed my purse and phones, and I was out the door.

Everything looked the same on the streets, so it was obviously just my night that had gotten me all fucked up. It took me half an hour to get to the docks, but once I got there I couldn't remember exactly where we'd been.

"Excuse me?" I called to a fisherman.

"Where is the yacht called Payback?"

For my effort, I got a shake of the head and shoulders, but no directions. Figuring it wouldn't be too hard to spot, I made my way up and down the docks looking for Rah and the boat. The longer I looked, the more I got a bad feeling, which eventually led me to the Harbor Master's office.

"I hate to bother you, but I can't find the boat I came in on," I said, slightly embarrassed.

"No problem, Miss, what's the name of it?" he asked.

"The Payback."

"Okay, let me check our records. Ah, here it is right here. Well, it was here."

"What do you mean *was* here?"

"It seems to have set sail last night sometime."

"That's not possible," I replied, shaking my head.

His response was to turn the computer monitor around where I could see it. Sure enough, it said The Payback had sailed out of slip seven-sixteen at just after 1 a.m. That made no goddamn sense though! *Where was Raheem? Had someone hurt him and taken the boat? What the fuck was going on?*

CHAPTER EIGHTEEN

"How do you feel?" he asked.

"I'm fine. What about you?"

"As long as you're good, I'm good."

"Really, JR? I understand how much prison forced me to numb myself to feelings in general, but you don't have to be that way," I told him.

"Mom, every day you spent in prison I was right there with you. What hurt you, hurt me, and I was forced to bury a lot of my emotions as well. The family was always worried about me. Don't get me wrong because you know how much I love Uncle Joe and Aunt Florine, but I couldn't share my pain with them. I couldn't share it with anyone because only one person could understand. You."

I searched his eyes for the truth, believing that he meant what he'd said, but still knowing he'd just seen me do something horrible to his father. This plan of justice may have started out as his idea, but this wasn't hypothetical anymore, and it was only gonna get worse.

"You know, now that I'm home I can finish the rest of this by myself. You've done enough to help me, baby," I told him, taking his hand in mine.

We were sitting in back of the house since it faced nothing but the alley and a corner store about a half a block away.

"Do you remember that day when I came to see you and I demanded you tell me the truth?" he asked softly.

I remembered that day like it was yesterday. As a parent we do our best to preserve and protect our child's innocence for as long as possible. But in the hood, the streets talk and kids will listen to what they have to say closer than devoted Christians will a Sunday sermon. It had been a long time since I'd done what I'd done, but nobody forgot. Back then JR was still going by LJ because he hadn't known what his father had done to his mother. But once he turned twelve, the questions started. I put him off as long as I could, but on his thirteenth birthday he demanded the full story.

"I remember, baby," I replied, squeezing his hand.

"After you told me the truth nothing was ever the same, but I had no regrets. I don't think I ever loved you more than that day. At the same time, anything I felt about my father or that side of his family died. I know that wasn't your intention at all Mom, but you deserved better than that, so much better. I'm saying all this to say that everything that comes next is okay with me because they brought it on their damn selves."

I fought the tears I wanted to shed for my baby boy, for all he'd lost while I was away. I knew he didn't want my tears, he wanted me to be happy, and he wanted the cycle to be complete.

"I understand, sweetheart. So, what's next?" I asked.

"Well, if I'm right then Shayna will be on her way home soon so we should probably make sure everything is in place."

"If that's the case then we should check on everyone before we roll out the welcome wagon. Is ole boy gonna meet us at the spot?"

"Yeah, by the time we finish up here he should already be there waiting on us," he replied.

"How's the footage on your phone?"

"Clear."

"A'ight, let's wrap this shit up and get on to the main event. I can't wait.

Meanwhile in the Bahamas…

I was running around like a chicken with her head cut off, but I wasn't getting any answers or help for my efforts. The cops said I couldn't report Raheem missing because he could've easily left on his own, despite my millions of attempts to explain he wouldn't do that. We were getting married for fucks sake! There's no way he would just leave like that, not under his own free will.

I'd heard all types of stories about piracy in international waters and shit, and that yacht was definitely worth more than a few dollars! *What was I gonna do? What the fuck could I do?* Feeling useless and helpless were not things I was accustomed to, by any stretch of the imagination, I'm a goddamn boss!

Right now I just felt like a fish out of water. I tried again to call both Melissa and my mother, but their phones just rang a million times before the answering machine picked up.

I was so tired of talking to machines! I'd lost track of how many messages I'd left them, say nothing of Raheem and Cliff. I sure would've liked to know what the fuck had everybody so busy, but at the moment I needed to figure out what my next move was gonna be. Looking for the nigga felt more like looking for a needle in a haystack rather than actually attempting to do something productive.

What was the alternative? Leave? How could I do that not knowing where he was, or if he was alright? All I knew at that moment was sitting in this hotel room wasn't getting shit accomplished, and I was tempted to smoke another blunt of that killer. Maybe I'd wake up and the world would make sense again. I swear I'd never needed my mother's advice more in life than at this exact moment.

Closing my eyes, I tried to channel her, willing her voice to speak to me from a great distance. After a solid five minutes I realized I might be bat-shit cray-cray. There was only one sensible thing to do. Go home.

Grabbing my bags from underneath the bed I took the weed out and stashed it underneath the sink, figuring somebody would stumble up on a nice surprise. Gathering all my shit, I checked out of my room, popped into the gift shop for a duffel bag to carry everything in, and then got a taxi to the airport. What I needed right now was a little luck that I could catch a flight to DC today because I wasn't trying to be stuck anywhere that had weird shit going on.

"I need a one-way ticket to Regan National airport," I said, once I'd reached the ticket counter.

"Okay, Ma'am, let me see what we have for you. Will that be first class or coach?"

"First class."

"Okay. Well, we have one flight leaving in thirty minutes, but it only has coach seats available. If you want first class, then you'll have to wait until tomorrow."

I wanted to smack the shit out of this little black girl. She saw me standing here with my bag ready to go so why give me the option if my flight ain't until tomorrow? Common sense was hard to come by.

"I'll take the coach," I replied, sliding her my black card.

I wonder what would've happened if I'd asked to rent a jet. One thing this taught me though was the benefits of spoiling myself, and as soon as I got home, I was gonna have Melissa buy me a plane. I wouldn't do the GVI just yet, but I was way beyond Commercial commuting.

"I'm sorry, Ma'am, your card has been declined," the ticket girl informed me.

"Yeah right, you better swipe that again, Slim. Blow on the mufucka like an old fashioned Nintendo game or something. That's a black card, you don't just get one of those by accident."

"I tried three times," she whispered, obviously feeling bad for the looks I was getting. There was no way my shit wasn't good. My options in this moment were to show my natural ass and make a scene, or pay cash for the ticket.

"How much is the ticket?" I asked.

"Four hundred and eight dollars."

The thought of my black card not covering four hundred dollars was mind numbing, but right here wasn't the place to fix it.

I dug the cash out of my purse, paid for the ticket, and proceeded on through the terminal to my gate. Somebody somewhere had made a mistake, and as soon as I got home somebody's helmet was gonna roll for this shit. I sat, pissed off in silence, until they called us to board the plane. I tried to figure out how I'd gone from living in la-la land at this time yesterday to this bullshit now. Talk about bad luck!

Thankfully, the flight home was uneventful and peaceful, but the bullshit started again as soon as I got off the plane. Nobody was answering their goddamn phones, and it took me twenty minutes before I could reach Twan to come pick me up. I don't think I exhaled a sigh of relief until my Jag pulled up to the curb.

"You won't believe the shit I've been through youngin!" I said, sinking into the soft butter leather seats.

"Only you could manage to get into some shit on your vacation. Damn, three weeks wasn't enough to kick back and chill?" he asked, pulling off into traffic.

"Man, it was cool, but the last twenty-four hours have been hella crazy."

"What happened?"

I spent the rest of the ride bringing him up to speed, listening to just how weird it all sounded coming out of my mouth. It didn't matter though because at the end of the day, I was gonna use all my resources to find my man. I just prayed he was alright.

"I'll carry your bag up," Twan offered when we pulled up in front of my building.

I was too tired to argue, and actually grateful when he grabbed it and followed me to the elevator. My tub was calling me; I could hear it already, along with the blunt and bottle of Hennessy I needed.

"You want a drink?" I asked when I opened the door. I didn't hear his response because the scene I was walking into had my brain completely scrambled.

"What the fuck?"

"Welcome, Shayna. Come join Raheem on the couch," she suggested. I knew the face, but I couldn't place it. I had a moment of indecision, but the gun I suddenly felt in my back made up my mind.

"Twan, what are you doing?" I asked.

"My name ain't Twan, it's JR.

CHAPTER NINETEEN

"I don't give a fuck what you're calling yourself, you better get that goddamn gun out of my back! Nigga, I know your momma," I warned, still not sure what the hell was going on in my own house.

"Oh, you know his mom?" the woman standing in front of me asked, feeling more unease then relief at seeing that Raheem was in one piece.

"Take a seat, Shayna, and all will be explained to you," the woman said again.

This situation was all wrong, but I didn't see a way out of it that didn't include a bullet playing tag with my spine. I stepped forward into the living room and sat next to Rah. I could feel him shaking, despite the fact we weren't touching, and that sent the first waves of real fear to my heart. Rah wasn't no bitch, so if he was scared then it was probably a good idea to take this shit seriously.

"JR, give her your phone," the woman ordered.

I still couldn't place her face, but I felt like I should know who she was. You would think the huge scar starting at the left side of her throat that almost wrapped around the other side would be unforgettable. Someone had tried to cut her head off, but it had been a while ago, because the scar was puffy and healed. I took the phone then looked at her for further instruction.

"Watch the video."

I did as I'd been instructed but it took a minute to make sense of what I was actually seeing. As soon as I saw Lorenzo trapped down I should've looked away, but I didn't, I couldn't. He was begging and pleading for his life, and with each sob that came from him, I felt the chills running through my body get colder and colder.

157

The woman who was now standing in my living room was on video explaining to Zo that he had to answer and atone for his sins. She said that in the end everyone had to atone for what happened. The next thing I knew, the boy I knew as Twan, my trusted driver, put a razor to my son's dick and sliced it off without hesitation. Then he put it in Zo's mouth, muffling his screams, only a little. For untold minutes they stood there and watched him bleed, and listened to him scream, until she finally filled his body with bullets. My son was gone, he was really and truly dead this time, and the pain I felt now was real.

"Why?" I asked, looking at her through my tears.

"Maybe if I introduced myself it would all make better sense. My name is Makayla Preston. The man holding you at gunpoint is Lorenzo Thompson JR."

"That can't be," I mumbled, holding my head to stop it from exploding.

"Oh, but it is. You probably thought I was dead, right? Well, the truth is I did try to kill myself in the courtroom that day. I didn't see how I could go on living with the death sentence of the aids virus pumping through my veins. But as they say, if you wanna hear God laugh then tell Him what you've got planned. I sent my baby to heaven because she didn't deserve the misery of living with this disease. I didn't either, but thanks to the tax payers, prisoners actually get the meds needed to fight HIV/Aids, and they kept me alive long enough to have my day of justice."

"What does this have to do with me?" I asked.

"The sins of your child are not simply his own. Everyone who could've changed him, but didn't, is now gonna have to answer for what he did to me. Look through the pictures in the phone and see if you recognize any one."

With trembling fingers, I began a slow scan of the photo gallery in the phone. The first was a picture of a little girl I didn't know, even though her eyes looked familiar. The second was a picture of Cliff bound and gagged, and I knew right then what direction this was headed. Continuing to scroll I saw Melissa in the same position, and lastly, my sweet, innocent mother. I felt the bile in my throat and I tried to fight it down, but it was too late; I puked all on the carpet and coffee table in front of me, not giving two fucks how it made me look. This crazy bitch had my momma and I needed her back safely or I'd never forgive myself.

"W-What do you want?" I asked, wiping my mouth.

"Haven't you been listening? I want justice!" she screamed at me.

"Okay, but killing everybody won't give you justice. Listen, I have a lot of money and-."

"*Had*, a lot of money," she interjected.

"What? What do you mean *had*?" I asked.

"Haven't you tried to use your credit cards yet?" she asked.

"I…" I had a bad feeling about his.

"You still haven't figured out Raheem's part in this have you?" she asked.

In all the chaos I'd forgotten about him, but I turned to him now in search for answers. He didn't need to say a word because the answer was in his eyes. The little girl on the phone was his, which meant that they'd used him to get to me. I understood his reasoning for playing me, but the pain of the betrayal and the lies were threatening to crush me. I felt like my spirit was broken.

"Was it all a lie, Rah?" I asked.

"Shay, I didn't have a choice-."

"I understand," I said, not wanting to stomach his excuses.

"Tell me how this is gonna work," I said, addressing Makayla.

"Well, there are some papers you need to sign to turn over your legit business and properties. I've already got the money you hid offshore, and I'm already in control of your girls working in both Canada and Amsterdam. Your cars, your penthouse, it's all mine, and as soon as you turn over the rest of your empire I'll give you your mother back.

"What about Cliff and Melissa?" I asked.

"Consider them collateral damage," she replied.

It was my opinion and experience that almost everybody from the streets who was about that life could tell a killer from a pretender. This bitch wasn't playing, so there was only one thing I could do.

"I'll do it," I agreed, handing JR his phone back.

"Good. Now we're all gonna go for a little ride."

Raheem and I were herded downstairs and into my car, neither of us so much as whispered for fear of causing our loved one's harm. I watched the city I loved pass by my window, wondering if anything would ever be the same again. I didn't feel like I could rebuild here, not unless I was prepared to go to war with Makayla and the rest of her family. *How would I live though? Was it too late to start over somewhere else?* These were all questions for after the situation was over, because right now, I had no guarantees.

Within thirty minutes, we pulled up in front of a plain white house. Once we were inside I could see that decorating wasn't a priority, which meant this was gonna be all business.

"Where's my daughter?" Rah asked as soon as we came through the door.

"We'll get to that," Makayla replied, leading us down a hall to the first door on the right.

Once we were all inside the room I noticed Cliff and Melissa bound and gagged on the plastic tarp covering the floor. The only furniture in the room was a desk that sat against the far wall, piled with papers. As soon as Melissa spotted me she was grunting and trying to roll towards me, but received a kick in the face for her efforts.

"We had your loving assistant draw up all the necessary paperwork, so now all you have to do is sign where ever you see an arrow and it'll all be over," Makayla said.

I made my way to the desk and signed everything without reading a word. Nothing material measured up to my mother. When I was done, I handed her the papers and she checked every single one, thoroughly.

"It was a pleasure doing business with you," she said, turning for the door.

I followed her out and we'd made it halfway down the hall when two shots rang out loudly. My knees buckled, but Rah was there to catch me, and as I looked behind us I saw JR closing the door to the room we'd just left.

The river of tears I was trying to see through were for both of the people I'd lost in that moment. I couldn't breakdown now though, so I made my feet move one in front of the other until we were standing next to Makayla, in front of the last door on the left.

She opened the door and there was my mother, huddled in a corner with Rah's little girl.

"Raheem, take your daughter and leave," Makayla ordered, pulling out a pistol of her own.

His daughter flew into his arms and held on tightly. Calling his name over and over, and begging to be taken home. When he looked at me I could see how torn he truly was, but this wasn't about me and him. A normal parent would do anything for their child, and I finally understood that.

"Go," I whispered to him, not willing to say good bye or the million other things I wanted to say. All I could hope was that he would be a good father to his little girl.

"Shayna, what's all this about?" my mother asked me, standing up.

"I'm sorry, Mom, it's my fault."

"Oh, you finally get that now?" Makayla asked, sarcastically.

"Yeah, I do."

"Too little, too late though."

"Who is this woman, Shay?" my mom asked.

"That's Makayla."

"Makayla… as in Lorenzo?"

"Yeah," I said, crossing the room to stand beside her.

"Young lady, your problem is with my grandson, not us-"

"You don't escape blame. If your daughter had been a better mother, or you a better grandmother, he may not have been such a fucked up individual," Makayla said.

"We did the best-."

"No. No I didn't, Mom. I was never the mother Lorenzo needed, and that's why he grew up hating women. You were a great mother to me, but I failed him."

"Shayna, all parents make mistakes, baby, we're humans too."

"Yeah, but my mistakes made a monster. Listen, Makayla, I know saying I'm sorry don't fix shit, but as a woman I understand how you feel."

"You think you understand how I feel?" she asked, laughing.

"Bitch, you chose not to raise your son, I lost the chance to raise mine! You have no fuckin' idea how I feel!"

"Hurting us ain't gonna make you feel better," my mom said.

"Oh, really? Let's find out," Makayla replied, grabbing my mom by the hair and forcing her to her knees.

"Makayla, wait!" Rah called out.

162

"You still her nigga? Do you and your daughter wanna die too? JR show him to the door, and if he hesitates shoot him."

"Makayla, I've given you everything you asked for, you don't have to hurt my mom," I reasoned. She looked me in the eyes and I thought she'd keep her word to let us go. But there was a madness in her eyes that left me with an empty feeling.

"Because of your family I lost a lifetime, and my life. You'll always owe me, so consider this me collecting."

I didn't get to utter a word before she pulled the trigger, and I couldn't stop myself from lunging towards her. I was only inches from her when I felt the heat of a thousand sins in my chest and then I was looking at the cracked plaster on the ceiling. The pain rendered me speechless, and I couldn't run even as I saw her looming over me.

"You should've had an abortion," she said. That was the last thing I heard before the hammer dropped.

The End

Coming Soon from Lock Down Publications/Ca$h Presents

TORN BETWEEN TWO

By **Coffee**

LAY IT DOWN **III**

By **Jamaica**

GANGSTA SHYT **III**

By **CATO**

BLOOD OF A BOSS **IV**

By **Askari**

BRIDE OF A HUSTLA **II**

By **Destiny Skai**

WHEN A GOOD GIRL GOES BAD **II**

By **Adrienne**

LOVE & CHASIN' PAPER

By **Qay Crockett**

I RIDE FOR MY HITTA **II**

By **Misty Holt**

THE HEART OF A GANGSTA **II**

By **Jerry Jackson**

<u>Available Now</u>

RESTRAING ORDER **I & II**

By **CA$H & Coffee**

LOVE KNOWS NO BOUNDARIES **I II & III**

By **Coffee**

LAY IT DOWN **I & II**

By **Jamaica**

PUSH IT TO THE LIMIT

By **Bre' Hayes**

BLOOD OF A BOSS **I II & III**

By **Askari**

THE STREETS BLEED MURDER **I, II & III**

By **Jerry Jackson**

CUM FOR ME

An **LDP Erotica Collaboration**

BRIDE OF A HUSTLA

By **Destiny Skai**

WHEN A GOOD GIRL GOES BAD

By **Adrienne**

A GANGSTER'S REVENGE **I II III & IV**

A SAVAGE LOVE 1

By **Aryanna**

WHAT ABOUT US **I & II**

NEVER LOVE AGAIN

THUG ADDICTION

By **Kim Kaye**

THE KING CARTEL **I, II & III**

By **Frank Gresham**

THESE NIGGAS AIN'T LOYAL **I, II & III**

By **Nikki Tee**

GANGSTA SHYT **I &II**

By **CATO**

THE ULTIMATE BETRAYAL

By **Phoenix**

DON'T FU#K WITH MY HEART **I & II**

By **Linnea**

BOSS'N UP **I & II**

By **Royal Nicole**

I LOVE YOU TO DEATH

By Destiny J

I RIDE FOR MY HITTA

By **Misty Holt**

BOOKS BY LDP'S CEO, CA$H

TRUST NO MAN

TRUST NO MAN 2

TRUST NO MAN 3

BONDED BY BLOOD

SHORTY GOT A THUG

A DIRTY SOUTH LOVE

THUGS CRY

THUGS CRY 2

TRUST NO BITCH

TRUST NO BITCH 2

TRUST NO BITCH 3

TIL MY CASKET DROPS

RESTRAINING ORDER

RESTRAINING ORDER 2

Coming Soon

TRUST NO BITCH (KIAM EYEZ' STORY)

THUGS CRY 3

BONDED BY BLOOD 2

IN LOVE WITH HIS GANGSTA

Aryanna

www.ingramcontent.com/pod-product-compliance
Lightning Source LLC
Chambersburg PA
CBHW070036260626
47159CB00005B/2053